PRAISE FOR CUI

"Hudson has shown... cryptozoology cases in the Sooner State, especially as it relates to Bigfoot."—Loren Coleman (cryptomundo.com), author of *Mysterious America* and *The Copycat Effect*

"Hudson takes you on an exciting journey…"—*Oklahoma Today*

"Hudson does an amazing job…you won't be disappointed."—Ravanne Alexander, Raven Guard Press

"[Hudson] did a fantastic job!"—Terri French, author *Tulsa's Haunted History*

"[Strange State] is great!!! I loved reading it... The writing style is very fun to read. I love the mixture of suspense and humor."—Darline Massie, Norman Public Schools

PRAISE FOR MARILYN A. HUDSON:

"Marilyn uses a darkly poetic writing style to create atmospheric, character-driven stories. The result: chills and a need to read the next."—Keith Pyeatt, award winning author of *Struck* and *Dark Knowledge*

"[She] has a way of captivating your senses and making you feel the emotions of her characters. The Bones of Summer demands your attention and leave you wanting more." –Terri French White, author of *Tulsa's Haunted Memories*

"[Hudson] blends her passion for history, libraries, books and stories to present a wide variety of tales."—*Norman Transcript*

"…Hudson's stories rule the night!"—Kathryn Thurman, storyteller

"Marilyn Hudson's writing is enticing and dynamic, each story unfolds cinematically."—Max Tell, author *The Land of Gnaws*

Books by Cullan Hudson

*Strange State: Mysteries and
Legends of Oklahoma*

Books by Marilyn A. Hudson

*Elephant Hips Are Expensive
The Bones of Summer
When Death Rode The Rails
Hell's Half Acre*

Copyright © 2011 Whorl Books
All Rights Reserved

No part of this book may be reproduced or utilized in any form or by any means, electronic or mechanical, including photocopying, recording or by any information storage and retrieval system without permission in writing.

Address inquiries:

Whorl Books
5658 NW Pioneer Circle
Norman, Oklahoma 73072

First Edition

Cataloguing-in-Publication Data

The Mound / Written by Cullan Hudson and Marilyn A. Hudson. Norman, Oklahoma: Whorl Books, 2011.

Summary: A psychic, an archaeologist, and an architect wage battle against an ancient evil haunting an old hotel in the mysterious town of Corvus Mound, Oklahoma.

1. Oklahoma – Fiction – Adult. 2. Supernatural – Oklahoma – Fiction.
3. Ghosts – Fiction- Adult.
I. Hudson, Marilyn A. II. Hudson, Cullan.

ISBN 1463755783 Pbk
ISBN-13 9781463755782
E
PZ 7

Printed in the United States of America. Layout, illustration and design by Cullan Hudson / Fresh Eire Design

Marilyn A. Hudson dedicates this work to her family, especially the memory of Lou, Velma, Roy and Carol.

Cullan Hudson dedicates this work to Jeff

SOUTHERN OAKS

METROPOLITAN LIBRARY SYSTEM
"SERVING OKLAHOMA COUNTY"

"I propose, therefore, to examine the evidence, fragmentary and moot though it is, of possible precursors of Columbus."
—Constance Irwin, *Fair Gods and Stone Faces*

"History is the version of past events that people have decided to agree upon."
—Napoleon Bonaparte

"Hell is empty and all the demons here...."
—William Shakespeare, *The Tempest*

"Do not speak of evil for it creates curiosity in the hearts of the young."
—Lakota Proverb

"When good people in any country cease their vigilance and struggle, then evil men prevail."
—Pearl S. Buck

a novel

PROLOGUE
Eastern Oklahoma, 1912

The trio of miners worked relentlessly inside the tunnel's gaping, inky maw. The jaundiced light sputtering from their lanterns could scarcely penetrate the unnatural blackness of the tunnel. Hour after hour, the staccato rhythm of their tools took them deeper into the hillside.

Wiping the sweat from his eyes, Andrew realized this was the farthest he, Frank, and Miguel had come during their work. It should have been reason to celebrate; they were, after all, nearly halfway finished. However, something about the job did not sit well with him—it never had. It became apparent after they found the first artifacts that this massive earthen knoll was obviously an old Indian mound and not a coal-rich hill. Andrew felt uncomfortable desecrating anyone's final resting place and could not understand why they had been ordered to dig here.

Compounding his uneasiness was the realization that only they three had been ordered to work this shaft. Usually, entire teams worked one tunnel. He had to wonder. It was no secret that workers such as himself, hired out for a few days, were often expendable. Mining in these parts was dangerous business. Nor did it help that only yesterday he'd had it out with the boss.

The owner was a short, plump man named Jonathan O'Malley who would only meet the men outside the tunnel entrance where he would stand, gnawing on a cigar. His two beady, green eyes flickered constantly from within a face mottled permanently by either the sun or his frequent bellowing outbursts.

The old man always seemed to be searching out that next blunder that would trigger his legendary Irish temper. In fact, lately everyone around these parts seemed to be walking the edge, barely controlling a mother lode of hot anger.

So here they were, a tiny odds-and-ends crew working secretively, long after most other shifts had ended. Three men scratching like moles in the grime and darkness of an eastern Oklahoma hillside. Andrew wondered what the other two men might have done to end up down here.

He knew little about the men slinging dirt and rock beside him. He only knew Frank was a farm boy who read a lot but daydreamed even more; whereas Miguel was passing through, just marking time until he had saved enough to move on.

As Andrew plowed away, he felt the wall in front of him abruptly give way. A few seconds later, its center collapsed inward with a shower of brown dust.

His heart thudded to a stop and didn't seem to start back up for many seconds. Andrew was sure the next sound would be a cave-in, trapping them under tons of earth. When the dust finally settled and the ground stopped moving, he urgently called to the others.

Frank and Miguel ran forward to gather around the collapsed wall. He could see his own earlier fear reflected in their wide eyes and heaving chests. The collapse had formed an opening in the tunnel and what lay beyond was a dark void.

"Frank, grab the lantern," Andrew urged. "There's a cave here!"

Frank, returning with the lantern, tossed it to Andrew leaning inside the newly formed opening.

"Careful, Andrew," Frank urged. "You don't know how secure that wall is."

"It'll be all right," Andrew assured. "I'm just going to take a peek. Miguel, bring your light over here."

Inside the opening, their feeble lamps revealed a room-sized cavity where pale objects lay scattered throughout the chamber. Peculiar stone pillars, ornately carved, stood like sentinels in the corners. Amid littered jumbles of rock and dirt, lay shards of pottery, beadwork, and nearly desiccated baskets. An even more oddly shaped object lay prominently on a stone slab in the center of the chamber.

Miguel quickly crossed himself and backed out, muttering something in Spanish. He indicated to Frank and Andrew that he had no intention of going back inside. Andrew, however, was curious and ventured further into the chamber. Frank scrambled in behind him, playing his light along the walls.

"Look at the walls," Frank exclaimed in awe. "There's writing or drawings or something."

Andrew lifted his lantern to add its light to Frank's as they silently searched the closest rock face.

Faint white spirals, deep notched lines, and geometric shapes ringed the chamber wall. There were also drawings of human-like figures, hulking beasts, and things he couldn't even begin to describe. Each figure was more grotesque than the last, but all seemed to scurry about in the pale, flickering light.

Now that the dust had settled, Andrew's eyes could fully adjust to the gloom. A large slab sat slightly askew near the center of the chamber piled with more rock and litter. After a moment's pause, he drew closer. Lifting the light over his head, Andrew now more fully realized what he was witnessing. Atop the slab were piled more objects, concealed beneath the crumbling remnants of a thin, stained cloth. Tiny beads still clung to the aged fabric by fragile threads.

He glanced back at Frank who stood behind, trying to get a better look. He could tell by the expression in Frank's eyes that they were thinking the same thing: Treasure!

Andrew inhaled sharply as he drew the cloth away. No silver or gold. Instead, under the cloth they came face to face with the desiccated remains of some hideously deformed man—if it could be called a man.

"God almighty!" Andrew cried, flinching at the hollowed eyes and gnarled brown teeth that sat framed by lips shriveled back into some horrid mockery of a smile.

"What is it?" Frank shouted as he peered over Andrew's shoulder.

"It's a body! It's all dried out and...."

"Deformed."

"Look at the size of him!" Andrew ran his eyes down the mahogany form. "Must be more than seven feet tall!"

Andrew's first cry had coaxed Miguel back into the chamber. Driven as much by concern as curiosity, Miguel clamored over the uneven floor to stand beside the others.

"What is this place?" he wondered aloud. "I don't like it here. Let's go!" Then he saw the form resting atop the stone slab. "Madre de Dios! What is that thing?!"

"A mummy!" Frank replied as he smiled up at Miguel with youthful exuberance. "It's gotta be one of those mummies I read about."

Andrew cautiously fingered an ornate necklace that lay askew atop the body's sunken chest. "Do you think that stuff there is gold?"

Frank gently removed the cloth from the rest of the bones, spilling a small clay pot in the process. A puff of ancient dust burst from the shards. A moan, low and long, sighed through the shadowed cavern. The sound was like the wind rushing in and swirling around on a bitter winter day.

"Damn!" Andrew cursed. "Be careful!" He could feel the sweat on his body chill.

"This isn't right," Miguel voiced worriedly. "We shouldn't be messing with this. Let's get out of here now!"

"Just a moment, Miguel," Despite himself, Andrew felt curiosity blossoming. "This guy could be loaded with treasure."

"It's not worth it, Andrew," Miguel snapped, maneuvering toward the opening. "I'm leaving this place!"

"Come on," Andrew implored as he fingered the cryptic symbols scrawled along its edges. "Look at this jewelry and the stone he's lying on…. Those could be worth something."

"I've seen just about every kind of stone there is," Frank stated. "But this don't look like anything I've seen."

The stone's dark surface had been finished to a mirror-like polish, which captured their faces and distorted them into twisted caricatures.

The cavern was rapidly filling Miguel with dread. Its stuffy, fetid air pressed in around him. Frank and Andrew, however, were completely transfixed by their find. Miguel briefly toyed with the idea of leaving the two men behind, but he seemed unable to tear himself away.

Something swooped past the men in the darkness behind them. Worriedly they looked around, but their eyes were drawn back to the strange sepulcher.

After a few minutes, though, Andrew slowly became aware of several peculiar sensations. Despite the heat, a series of sudden chills coursed through him, turning the sweat on his face and back to ice water. His heart thudded erratically in his chest, and he felt the room envelop him in a suffocating embrace. Wiping sweaty palms down his grimy shirt, Andrew wheezed in small breaths of air, which seemed to have grown as thick as oil in his chest.

The men never shook their gaze from the strange corpse atop the mirrored stone until an abrupt cry broke the spell. Frank and Andrew dragged their eyes back toward Miguel who was moaning plaintively in Spanish. His dark eyes wildly searched the chamber. Then they too became aware of the sound.

A low thrum filled the void, permeating their bodies like an electric charge. Even as Andrew tried to focus on its source, the sound changed to a harsh, excruciating drone that set his nerves on edge with every pulse and brought a gasp of pain.

Frank covered his ears as he stumbled blindly toward the opening, desperate to escape the sound.

Spinning around in a daze, Andrew peered into the gloom, but he could not pinpoint the sound either. It was everywhere.... It was nowhere.

In a panic, he suddenly realized he could not find the entrance anymore. Think! He told himself as he fought off the pain, but the sound filled the chamber like a flood of murky water, turning the world upside down. He felt disoriented, adrift on a river of confusion. Its unceasing pressure fogged his thoughts with each passing second.

"Where's the opening?" Andrew shouted to the others, who had now fallen to their knees upon the floor. His words were swallowed by the noise.

The space filled with their low pained mutters. Their cries reflected his own growing torment as he cradled his head. The hot auger drilling into his skull made everything else disappear no matter how he struggled. Staying on his feet grew more difficult with each passing moment.

Dark shadows swirled around him, leaving intense pain in their wakes.

In the faint lantern light, he could see dark rivulets of blood streaming from Miguel's ears and nose as a pained grimace warped his face. Andrew could see Frank ripping out handfuls of hair as he thrashed insanely before falling heavily to the floor.

Inside Andrew's head, the pain was intense. There was nothing but the pain.

Spinning around once more in a frantic, desperate attempt to locate the chamber entrance, Andrew lost his footing and crumpled to the floor. He fought to stand against the pressure in his head, but the force drained him of the power.

Shadows brushed against him and he winced, feeling his skin being slashed in the darkness. He was dying. He was dying in a world of pain so incredible that he lost all awareness of anything before and sensed there would be nothing after.

For a brief instant, his dwindling consciousness caught the silhouette of a tall figure framing the ragged chamber opening. Some part of him wanted to reach out and grasp the figure, to plead for help. Then, as pain like molten rock seared through his body, he screamed one last time before collapsing.

Outside the entrance to the chamber, the tall man stooped to draw a series of symbols in the dirt. The men in the chamber now lay dead. The bone-jarring hum had retreated to a barely audible murmur, but it still lurked along the chamber's dark periphery, a predator waiting in the shadows. The man paid no attention.

Pulling a small clay flask from his back pocket, the stranger carefully lifted it high at the mouth of the chamber. Then, in a language long-forgotten by most, he chanted rhythmically, "hilka, hilka, besha, besha..."

The humming inside the chamber increased as he poured the last of the contents across the opening. The dark, oily substance beaded briefly atop the soil before the puddles suddenly came to life, snaking sinuously across the cavern entrance. After a moment, the dirt steamed before the liquid slowly leeched into the tainted soil at last.

Standing, the man hefted a spool of fuse wire. Carefully he retraced his steps through the main tunnel.

Once at the entrance, the man wrapped the fuse around the support beams and dashed into a copse of nearby trees. Moments later, the earth gave a fierce, convulsive shrug as the dynamite exploded and plumes of dirt erupted from the tunnel entrance.

Lifting his weary arm, the man wiped the sweat from his dark face. The chamber was sealed once again in the sunken rubble of the ancient mound. More importantly, so was the malevolence it held. The tomb surely was now a tomb once more, sealing away that which should not be revealed—could not be revealed. Not again.

1

Death wore a gray hooded sweatshirt when he rudely jostled Shade Hoffmeyer on the sagging old porch. He only touched her in a psychic sense, but the reality of it was so powerful that she nonetheless staggered awkwardly from the impact. With a start, she turned to follow him as he vanished down the rain-sodden Seattle street.

This one's strong.

Shade brushed several errant strands of long, dark hair from her face. Though some might have been hard-pressed to see it, beneath her stark, goth appearance, the twenty-three-year-old was quite beautiful.

Unlike most who donned similar attire, Shade wasn't all ennui and bad vampire novels.

She possessed complicated layers that not even her most intimate acquaintances knew. She cultivated the stringent look more as a barricade to those who would otherwise wish to get too close.

She spent most days running a small software company, which afforded her the skills to design custom applications for her NetFone. She could download that hot new track or refresh herself on the proper way to conduct a Tibetan cleansing ritual. At the moment, nothing as ambitious as that was required of her device. Instead, she jotted down a few thoughts concerning the presence she had just encountered.

Stepping down from the old porch, Shade walked into the soft mist, heedless of the rain drizzling down on her. She was intent only upon seeing the figure as he disappeared from view.

No use. He was gone.

Turning swiftly, Shade surprised the two men waiting for her back on the porch. A sudden vision of herself as she must look to them made her want to laugh: long, wet hair, black biker boots, and a vintage t-shirt clinging damply to her chest. She gathered her floor length coat around her like a cloak and strode forward.

Detectives Roy Wilcox and Henry Ruiz paused, shuffling awkwardly. They wondered why she had lagged behind to gaze down the dismal, water-logged streets. They did not know that what she had seen standing there on the crumbling porch, with a cold and constant mist falling, was an earlier day awash in a brilliant blue sky and the rustle of wind-tousled trees.

In her mind, she had seen the day a killer found his own bizarre form of happiness in the savage ruin of an innocent young girl.

With his bulky frame and grizzled, gray hair, Wilcox reminded Shade of a teddy bear. His partner, Ruiz, however, seemed more like an oily sewer rat.

Different in looks and representing opposing viewpoints on a dozen subjects—including Shade's presence—the men nonetheless shared a common vision: They would move and work as one to find the person who had kidnapped, killed, and dumped the body of a delightful fourteen-year-old named Sarah Crane in this house over a month ago.

Had the others been able to see the man, he would have appeared simply as another lanky young fellow with no cares, scarcely worth noticing. There was a spring to his step as he whistled a lively, off-key tune. He was in good spirits because he had just done some of his most satisfying work in the small house.

However, in his wake, he left fuming black footprints that only she could follow. Each step seemed to flare and sizzle before dissolving into vapor. The images were vivid and coming at her with great speed: manifestations of both the man's nature and his actions.

She knew this from past experience, but she could also sense the remnants of his mood as well as his mind. This one was bad. Wherever this man walked, he would leave a trail of death.

It had been a long time since she had reacted so powerfully to a location. It made her both very curious and very cautious. What might she encounter once she was actually inside the house where he had played?

Entering the home, Shade found herself slowing again. Passing through the thick, humid air was like tearing through Hallowe'en spider webs that tugged her in strange directions. It was not really the air, though. It was a psychic fog that permeated the crime scene. It was in this haze that her mind was seeking answers. She could feel the dull throb in the back of her head—the one that said she would pay for this later.

Why can't I get a hangover the normal way, she mused mirthlessly, massaging her neck.

Shade stepped gingerly through the living room, skirting missing floorboards. Thoughtfully, she tugged at the massive spiked collar she always wore. She closed her eyes. She could hear faint scratching sounds. She sniffed at an air redolent of wet dog, rotting wood, pungent molds, and waste products she did not even want to think about. Shade could not imagine a worse place to die.

Wilcox carried a folder in one burly hand. Shade knew from working with him before that it would contain pertinent details of the victim, crime scene photos, and every small lead they had followed.

The trio entered what had once been a bedroom. Bare walls with gaping holes revealed the old lathe slats beneath. The atmosphere was dusty and decayed. The water-stained ceiling bulged downward, straining to remain in place. Everywhere, windows were broken out and boarded up and broken out again.

Shade stared at the floor for a long moment as images flashed before her eyes. She wouldn't need the crime scene photos because she could see it all.

"She was found tied up here." Wilcox said, his voice making a low, gravely sound as if he were choking on each syllable. He always took it personally when a child was killed. "Gagged. Her throat slashed with some kind of—"

His voice thickened to a whisper as insubstantial as the shadows that painted each corner of the old house. Shade knew those were only some of the things that had been done to the young girl.

"Someone called it in," his partner added. "Patrol unit checked it out and found the body. They saw the floor and it seemed obvious what had gone down."

Shade took another look at the floor where the detective pointed. Roughly in the center was painted a large, crudely shaped pentagram. Its blood red surface had worn off in places.

"The pentagram." Wilcox said, staring at the floor. "The one we told you about."

"Roy, let the lady work."

Shade recognized the code for don't tell her too much. She also knew Ruiz did not support the family's decision to call her in to review the case. Like most, he did not trust psychics and suspected a con. After nearly two months with no leads, however, he was being what was, for him, extremely tolerant.

"It's cut and dried, Henry. It has been from the start. That thing on the floor tells the whole story. This was some kind of satanic cult. Some ritualistic freaks."

"Now, Roy, you know there was a lot of drug related activity going on here as well...."

The two men fell into the comfortable, and probably comforting, mock argument on the merits of one theory or another. Arguments that reaffirmed their place in the normal and sane world.

Shade left them to it and focused instead on drawing on the floor. Stooping down, she ran her fingers over the design where the paint was thickest. A faint sound came to her from the muffled recesses of another time. A breathy whistle of a tune performed slightly off-key, whispering not from the floor but from the hallway.

She walked back out into the hall, following the tune into the kitchen. Nothing. But as she neared the bathroom....

Rub-a-dub-dub, so much blood in the tub....

He had definitely been here more than once, probably cleaned up here. He felt... comfortable here. It was familiar.

Yes.

She shadowed the killer's requiem cautiously down the hall, stepping gingerly back into the bedroom and opening the closet. The detectives fell silent, watching her as she into the dark abyss beyond the battered old door.

Yes, here...

"Detective Wilcox," Shade spoke up, suddenly drawing their attention. "The pentagram you can forget. Just booze, sex, and drugs. Small town wannabes playing at being big and bad. It's not connected to your killer. He saw it, though, and thought it would be funny to lay her body out like Da Vinci's *Vitruvian Man.*"

"See! I told you, Roy!"

Wilcox merely shrugged his shoulders at the smirk on his partner's face and continued to watch Shade.

"The satanic crap is just some dude's way of trying to get into his girl's pants. He didn't even draw it right. If it had been real, the *Animus*—the single point—would have been facing downward. The…*artist* just has a cheesy mustache and a penchant for 80's hair bands. So wipe Satanic cults off the suspect list."

"That's good, isn't it?" Wilcox asked. His haggard face lifted for a moment before he noticed she was still searching the corners of the room.

"Do you have one of those little evidence bags?" She grinned at the two men, "You know the type they always show on TV?"

Ruiz furrowed his brow as he slowly tucked his hand into a pocket, retrieving a small plastic bag.

"Inside the closet, just above the door, is a knife resting on the lintel. You're going to want that. It has his prints on it—and his blood. Maybe you can get some DNA."

"You're sure?" Wilcox asked with a tinge of doubt. Yet even as he asked, he was already digging out plastic gloves and an evidence bag.

"Yes." She stared, as if scrutinizing the emptiness in front of her. "He's getting more confident with each kill. Too confident, really. He doesn't think he'll get caught, and leaving evidence like this is his way of flaunting that."

Ruiz snapped on latex gloves and reached inside the door frame, feeling around for the knife she described. It was obvious by his expression that Ruiz had no expectation of finding it.

With a stunned expression and his hand frozen above his head, Ruiz stared back at Shade. Slowly, he brought down from the lintel a long kitchen knife, its blade stained dark red.

"Those prints will solve two other murders in nearby counties, and the evidence pulled from one of those will tie to this place. I don't know how, but it will."

Roy Wilcox stared in blank awe for a moment. Pulling out his notebook, he began to jot down all Shade had told him.

"Oh, and he has a connection to this place. He may have grown up here, or lived in this house once, or came over a lot. It felt like home to him."

"How do you know this?" Ruiz was now trying his best to loom over her in an intimidating fashion. Shade was sure it usually worked. He was small, but possessed the intensity of a much larger man.

She could not give him what he wanted. Truth was she had no clue how she knew; only that she did and was usually correct. Some people would never be convinced about what she did or why she did it. She had seen it all many times before. She had done what she could for the young girl here. It was up to men like these now.

That throb in her head was now turning into a drum solo. She had a feeling she knew what it meant. She needed to get out of here and find some place devoid of negative psychic residue.

A strange sound like a faraway waterfall caught her attention. Shade turned to see hundreds of crows fly through the room and out the door in one long, undulating stream. The detectives continued their tasks unaware of the avian torrent rushing *en masse* above their heads.

The throb in her skull became a steady hum of chilling intensity.

What's going on? This was a new wrinkle, but Shade knew from experience that whatever was happening would not bode well.

Silently, she watched as the birds swarmed out the door and vanished into the drizzle. She simply stared for a few moments as she contemplated this new development.

"Roy," she said finally as she turned to leave. "You called me just in time. When you pick him up, he will have plans for his next victim in his car. A twelve year-old with red hair."

Her cell phone buzzed, and the throb ended as abruptly as it had begun.

Giving the two men one last look, she flipped it open. "Kevin, what's up?"

"Planning anything big for Memorial Day weekend?" Kevin Anderson's voice sounded tinny over the cell phone.

Kevin had only come to know Shade a few years before when they both designed gaming software for the same firm. In time, they had amassed enough money to launch their own company, Byte Marks, which already boasted three top-selling titles.

Kevin also had the somewhat bewildering task of serving as her assistant when it came to, as she put it, "pimpin' her out to the man." He was a go-between in her dealings with law enforcement and bereaved clients. It had taken him a while to become convinced of her abilities. However, once he had, a whole new—sometimes unsettling—world had been opened up to him.

"What is it?" She asked, dreading what he had in mind.

"Well, I have your next gig," he began, pausing for any protestations. "A TV station over in Oklahoma is doing a documentary about a haunted hotel. They want a group of experts, including some psychics, to examine the site."

"No doubt the annual spook piece for the Hallowe'en season." Shade avoided the media as much as possible, preferring to work quietly with the police or family members. She did what she did and let the police take the credit. It was a system that served both parties well.

"I wonder how they found you."

"That's a good question, since I discourage…" Her voice trailing, Shade peered into the home's misty backyard. Seven fat crows had perched themselves along an old battered fence and stared directly at her. Shade shook her thoughts away. "Tell the station that's a no."

"You sure? They're paying a few grand."

"Yeah." Shade glanced out the window once more. The crows were gone.

"Okay. I can't imagine what kind of dump they'd be putting you up at in a place like…. What did she call it? Ah, Corvus Mound, Oklahoma."

Suddenly, her attention snapped back full-focus on her conversation with Kevin. Corvus… *Crows….*

"Where did you say this hotel was?"

"Uh…C-Corvus Mound," Kevin stammered slightly, bewildered by her sudden interest. "Why?"

"I'll fill you in later. Just tell them yes. Be clear that I want my face blurred or backlit or something."

Shade turned back to the two detectives who had waited patiently in the dining room. "Excuse me, gentlemen," she said as she gathered the coat around her. "Roy, you know how to get in touch. Ruiz, it was nice to meet you."

"You leaving town?" Roy Wilcox asked. She knew he would be genuinely sorry to see her leave.

"Yeah, have to talk to a man about a job." Hearing how that sounded, Shade nearly chuckled. Her freelance jobs were seldom anything to laugh about.

With a practiced hand, Shade deftly flipped the coat hood over her head. She moved toward the door, leaving the men with the eerie impression of a wicked Mona Lisa smile sunk deep within the shadows of a long, black cloak.

Creepy girl, thought both men silently.

In her head, she heard them. Their reaction was all she needed to make such an exit worth it. She laughed as she plodded down the steps.

"Was that over the top?"

****

Shade stared out the window of her Salt Lake City hotel.

Mechanical trouble grounded her flight home and she had been put up by the airline in an ancient rat trap near the airport. She barely noticed the orange carpet or the scent of Freon and nicotine fuming from the old rattling AC unit. Instead, she was focused on the images that had bolted her from another night's sleep. Since her encounter in Seattle the day before, she hadn't been able to sleep without the intrusion of dark, troubling dreams.

In these, she saw a hotel sitting plump and self-satisfied in a pool of brilliant sunshine. However, inside the hotel's labyrinthine halls, darkness and silence lay like a heavy blanket on a warm night. Its suffocating presence had been everywhere as she pushed herself through those dark corridors.

Then she was on a field of death, the stench of decaying bodies so strong Shade had to cover her nose and fight the nausea. The crimson sky roiled in the pyretic air. The only sounds were the hollow mourning of the wind and the harsh cries of crows in the distance.

Like rippling waves of hot air, a distortion to her left drew Shade's eyes. In seconds it resolved into the lanky brown form of a woman clad in ancient garb. She had two faces that oscillated rapidly, leaving her visage indistinct. Her mouths moved frenetically. Frustrated, she attempted to speak, but the sound was stolen by the hot desert wind and the raucous call of crows.

The birds rushed in, filling the sky and streaming across the barren, death-marred plain by the thousands. Shade ducked to avoid the razor-sharp claws and the onslaught of ebony wings.

The woman's voice finally broke through.

Come! The woman screamed, her words echoing and multiplying. *Come! Only you can help her!*

Shade knew it was no dream. It was impatient and demanding. Despite Shade's lack of understanding, the words continued coming to her psychically.

Come! Only you can help her!

To which Shade could only respond, "God! You are so annoying. Look, lady, this layover is completely out of my hands. You're just going to have to hold your horses or hell hounds or whatever."

2

Rick Donaldson stood before the large glass windows, looking down upon Boston's financial district. It was raining again. Daggers of lightning scarred the sodden sky, as thunder vibrated through the air.

The strains of Wolfram's aria *O! Du mein holder Abendstern* wafted over to him subtly from a Bose speaker hidden somewhere within his cavernous office. He didn't understand a word of German, but there was a sense of melancholic portent that seemed a fitting accompaniment to both the rainy weather and the events to come.

He closed his eyes and let his mind wander aimlessly on the music.

The door behind him opened with only the tiniest whisper. Morton Duncan entered as softly as a supplicant. Donaldson glanced at the Tag Heuer wrapped around his wrist, noting once more the man was as punctual as ever. In all his years working for the family, he had never seen Duncan arrive late.

"Ah, Duncan." He turned at last to face his family's private lawyer. Donaldson once more took note of the man's pale, almost cadaverous features and shuddered inwardly. The man may have been one of the best attorneys the family had ever known, but his cadaverous features were unsettling. "Have the papers been filed?"

Duncan dipped his head in a brief, patrician nod, revealing the careful training of a proper Oxford man.

"Yes, sir. The contracts are complete." He precisely arrayed several thick bundles of paper on the desk in front of Donaldson. "The members have been informed and Spencer is on the move."

"Let's hope he doesn't fail us again," Donaldson murmured as he signed each in turn.

He paused over the last name.

"The young architect is already hard at work, or so I have been informed by those watching him." Duncan added, noting Donaldson's attention to the last set of papers.

"Some of the members are concerned, however. They believe this is an unwise choice."

Donaldson glanced around the well-appointed office, seeing the framed images of him with nearly every scion of finance, politics, or entertainment worth mentioning. Nothing happened by chance, if he could help it, but he knew that at some point there was always a moment when chaos ruled and the outcome became uncertain.

"He's a gamble," Donaldson admitted. "But then it's all a gamble."

3

Juggling a cup of coffee and several drafting tubes, Matt kicked his foot back to shut the truck door, leaving a large, dusty boot tread. Glancing up, he examined the old hotel that loomed before him.

For almost a century, the Montford Arms had perched atop the hill forming the bulk of downtown Corvus Mound. Built in 1917, the hotel stood as a monument to a bygone era when opulence had been redefined by barons of industry with seemingly unlimited wealth.

The architect in Matt appreciated the clean lines of the red brick structure. Originally constructed as a ten-story rectangle, two wings were later added to the sides followed by four more floors. Its Renaissance Revival form had been executed masterfully; traces of Art Nouveau, Gothic Revival and hints of Art Deco framed the structure in a unique blend of styles.

Initially, the resort hotel was the only edifice atop the hill, a castle from which Silas Montford could rule. However, businesses soon hedged it in, shifting the commercial heart of Corvus Mound permanently.

Over the past century, the town around it had grown and then contracted, suffering through a depression, an oil bust, and six major military conflicts. Yet, through it all, the hotel had survived—even if it hadn't flourished. In that way, it reflected the community around it.

One of Matt's favorite spots was a small alcove on the top floor. From here, he could sip his coffee in peace while looking out across downtown as it spilled over the hill toward the southern half of Corvus Mound and the river that formed its eastern border. Following its sinuous, muddy-green course, as it meandered south toward the mounds, Matt could clearly see the bare tops of several larger mounds piercing the surrounding canopy.

Corvus Mound was obviously a survivor. If it was a little dilapidated around the edges, it at least fought valiantly to keep those corners out of sight. According to Donaldson—perhaps because of him—the local economy was surging once more and much of the view Matt now enjoyed would change as strip malls, chain restaurants, and those hotels that seemed to spring overnight from magic beans sprouted weed-like at its periphery.

Matt noticed a small, silver rental car parked in front of the hotel.

Damn!

He had hoped to get a little breathing space before Nancy arrived. Squaring his shoulders and taking a deep breath, Matt braced himself to meet his boss.

Nancy Rand reminded Matt of a fifty-seven year old tank in heels. Her fashionable ensembles only briefly disguised her thick skin and ruthless business savvy. He certainly respected his boss; she was an expert businesswoman. But she was also strident and quick to criticize.

After her husband's death, she had taken over his failing contracting business, turning it into a successful and highly-specialized enterprise known as Renewal Concepts, a Chicago-based company dedicated to hard-to-do or hardly-sought fixer uppers, particularly historic renovations. Renewal Concepts had grown in reputation over the years and now counted major museums and international royalty among its prestigious clientele.

While he found the work rewarding, Matt had begun thinking recently about leaving, perhaps starting his own company. It seemed like providence when Rick Donaldson walked into their offices with a phalanx of assistants and a mission to restore his family's turn-of-the-last-century hotel in the sleepy hamlet of Corvus Mound, Oklahoma.

Matt's hometown.

Although there was an obvious economic gap, he and Matt had seemed to hit it off instantly. Donaldson was only a few years older than Matt, which certainly bolstered their camaraderie, but they also shared this civil legacy. This, Donaldson explained, practically made them family.

If Matt had been a more cynical person, he might have reflected on how perfectly calculated these words seemed, given his personal history.

Matt's grandfather lived only twenty miles from Corvus Mound. Ben Yellow Wolf, however, had been more than that; he was the only true father Matt had ever really known.

Matt's own dad had been drunk, as usual, when he drove them both off the road in the Winding Stair Mountains. His father died instantly, but Matt lay injured and trapped for several hours. A faint scar still ran along his cheek like an indelible tear stain.

Afterward, his grandfather had taken in an angry, rebellious, and grief-stricken kid. Matt knew it could not have been easy. Matt had revolted against everything connected with his family.

He had refused to listen over the years as his grandfather, a Caddo elder, had tried to teach his beliefs, always talking about Matt's sacred lineage and destiny. Matt had tuned out all the nonsense about rituals and knew the old man had been deeply hurt by this rejection.

Matt also understood how much it had wounded his grandfather when he had shortened the family name to merely Wolf.

This trip was about more than just the instauration of an old hotel. It was also an effort to reconcile with a man Matt really did love despite all outward appearances of rejection.

Matt found himself perpetually enveloped by an expensive—and overly generous—cloud of *Clive Christian 1872* as he trotted to keep up with a power-walking Nancy Rand. As he should have expected, she had been early, barely growling a response to his greeting as he joined her in the lobby.

The heels of her Roger Vivier shoes clattered across the floor like machine guns as Nancy assaulted the hotel, barking orders and commanding her forces. She kept a running dialogue as she went and expected Matt to be right behind her like a dutiful dog, answering questions and following orders.

"Break it down for me."

"We were able to do a lot here with only minor re-furbishing," Matt said, indicating the main lobby and adjacent dining parlor. "Most of the lower floors have been completely renovated. We can open on schedule, finishing the upper floors one at a time."

"That's fantastic, but Donaldson has upped the opening date again."

Matt felt something vital wither and collapse in the pit of his stomach. He didn't understand Donaldson's urgency to open. The man certainly had the money to take the extra time to see things were done right. Overworked men got sloppy; accidents happened.

As they passed through the lobby, Matt took in the original columns of deep mahogany he had worked hard to save. They stood proudly, lifting high the richly carved ceiling, inlaid with panels of hand painted tin. He admired the exotic woods and weathered bronze once hidden beneath layers of grime.

A majestic staircase with red carpeting lolled from the dark chasm of the second floor like a tongue spilling from the mouth of some enormous beast.

"Well, we'll just have to do the rest with guests in residence," Matt suggested in weary tone. "Frank Sattler assures me his crew will be able to do those upper floors with a minimum of impact on the customers and the—"

"I get the picture," she said, holding up her hand as if a traffic cop. "Tell Sattler to contact the other subcontractors and get their crews here ASAP."

Renewal Concept's first order of business had been to assess the extent of the damage. In the case of this hotel's inner workings, they had caught up on over twenty years of bad plumbing, wiring, and structural issues. Bringing this all up to code required an army of specialized recruits.

The pair stopped at the landing to the lobby's grand staircase.

"Depressing, isn't it?" she asked.

Matt followed her eyes upward to the large carved relief depicting birds perched in sinister legion upon twisted branches.

"It is unnerving," he agreed. "Their eyes seem to follow me every time I pass."

"If I had my way," Nancy clucked, "that tacky thing would end up in the dump."

Matt knew her tastes ran more toward the sleek simplicity of modern décor. Perhaps she saw such futuristic minimalism as a charm to ward off encroaching age.

Now there's a catchy slogan, he thought. *You're only as old as your furniture.*

"But there's a lot to work with here." He attempted to inject a bit of optimism. It was, at times, difficult to understand how someone like Nancy Rand could be running a historical restoration company. "The reception counter, for instance, still has its original brass. It's a wonder this place wasn't stripped years ago."

"You're right there," Nancy noted. "Just think of trying to replace this opulent turn-of-the-century crap at today's rates."

"Somehow, I don't see money as a problem for our Mr. Donaldson."

"Speaking of which, I e-mailed you the amended time table."

"Understood."

"Oh, and brace yourself," she said with a dramatic pause. "It's confirmed: He's bringing in some group to film a special report for a TV station in Tulsa."

"When?" Matt groaned.

"Well, the one group," Nancy began as she consulted her notes, "will arrive mid-week, and then the rest come in on Friday."

"That soon?" Matt shook his head as he jotted this all down.

"Get some rooms ready, but don't worry much about the rest."

"We're cutting it close to get the project in on time as is."

"Well, they can work around us." Nancy told him. "Besides, it's Memorial Day weekend. None of the crew will be here anyway."

"I guess...." He still wasn't sure about all this. "We'll need to keep this group coming midweek out of the construction areas."

"Do what you need to do, Wolf. This is coming from Skippy himself."

Nancy had a low estimation of Rick Donaldson, whom she saw as another spoiled rich kid with more money than sense. He didn't work hard for his empire; it was handed to him, like this hotel he inherited from the Montford side of his family.

"Got it," Matt replied automatically. His mind was already drifting to the countless new chores now awaiting him.

"Anything else?" She asked while shutting her notebook, a move that conveyed she really didn't want any more headaches.

"Remember, you wanted some pictures? The local museum has a lot of old photos for the interior design team," he glanced at his notes, "I've made an appointment to meet with one of their administrators."

"Great," Nancy stated absently as she flipped open her notebook and sliced her pen across another item in her lengthy checklist.

"Well, we're not making money just standing around. We need to check out the—"

A soft buzzing bubbled up from somewhere in the depths of her leather handbag. A frown of irritation etched itself across her brow as she clawed through her purse to answer the cell phone. Within seconds she was barking at someone.

"That junk was to have been cleared out on Friday! Evidently you can't read a calendar because it is now Monday...."

Matt backed away gingerly and headed toward the kitchen. The further he walked through the cavernous corridors, the fainter Nancy's vitriol became. He could scarcely hear her strident voice as she berated whatever poor bastard made the mistake of calling her.

His solitude didn't last long. Moments later, he could hear her voice hunting him in the maze of rooms and corridors leading toward the kitchen.

"Wolf, there you are," Nancy said in exasperation, as if she had just spent the better part of an hour searching for him. "What about those paranoia windows Donaldson wants?"

"Yeah, what's with that?" Matt asked. "Is he expecting terrorists?"

"I know, I know," she clucked exasperatedly. "But it's his money."

"Well, they just finished installing the last of those today." He spoke as he followed Nancy back to the lobby. "I think he wants to boast about an added sense of safety in Tornado Alley."

"I can't imagine that's really a concern," Nancy proclaimed with a dismissive gesture.

"He seems to think it is—or his customers do. He also added the electronic security locks, which should be online later today."

"The rich are different from you and me," she spoke dryly, quoting F. Scott Fitzgerald.

Matt guessed it was probably on her quote-of-the-day calendar. Nancy wasn't known for her taste in classic literature.

"I'm going to check on the rest of this myself," She said as she started up the stairs to the second floor. "I need you to get with Sattler, and then check on those plumbers. I swear, if I have to...."

Mercifully her wrath was swallowed by the gloom as she ascended the grand staircase.

Shadows crossed the lobby floor and Matt glanced through the windows to the street beyond. Passing clouds obscured the faint sunlight, plunging the cavernous room into an icy shade. He shivered suddenly as a chill breeze brushed past him with a faint sigh that faded as quickly as it had appeared.

For reasons he couldn't understand, Matt felt a momentary sense of ennui wash over him in the depths of that shadow. As the sun emerged once more, the melancholy passed just as quickly.

He turned toward the rear of the building where the lead sub-contractor, Frank Sattler, was working downstairs in the kitchen.

As Matt arrived, Sattler was hitching his sagging jeans up his skinny hips and pointing to the blueprints spread out along the counter.

"This clears it up," Sattler stated unceremoniously. "There were two water wells. The one we know about was added in the fifties. The problem is the plans show another somewhere in the kitchen and we can't find it."

"The well opening was probably just covered and walled off." Matt offered.

"Pretty standard for the time." Sattler agreed. "I've seen it a dozen times in the past. The problem is that Corvus has some pretty particular rules about how you handle that kind of thing."

"What do we have to do?" Matt asked the older man.

"We have to locate that well and see it's up to code. That may mean tearin' a wall down in the kitchen. I know the city guy; I can get him on it right away."

Matt groaned as his mind readjusted time lines and budgets. "Good, we can't waste time on this one. I'll see you later, Mr. Sattler."

Striding away, he had visions of major delays and environmental paperwork. He made a note to call the authorities and see just what his alternatives were. Whose palms could he grease?

The hotel was his baby, all right. He only hoped it wasn't going to turn out to be a problem child.

4

She had underestimated the beast and such mistakes could kill. She had been careless in allowing it to trick her like that. Was she an old man or a silly child to let the creature turn her, a warrior of many battles, into the hunted?

She touched the hilt of her sword. Tracing its markings, she sought comfort in the power of the spirals carved there. Her mentor would have had her lashed for such a careless hunt.

She looked to the horizon where the brute was leaving a trail in the high grasses. She knew what must be done.

Images of the night flooded in, bringing a sharp stab of anger as she remembered how quickly the creature had struck and how terrible had been the toll. The priests had bound the beast, but before she and her sister could kill it, the creature tore through them like a ravenous dog. Now, the hunt was on.

The only sound was the whisper of the wind as it ran through the withered old fingers of nearby trees. Straining harder, she could only manage to pick up the faint murmur of the river as it cut through the landscape. The beast had grown as still and as quiet as death itself. She chided herself for briefly thinking that perhaps the creature had been more badly wounded than she first thought.

No, it was still out there, and she was certain with every fiber of her being that she was now the hunted and that—

Every muscle tensed as she spun around, sword tracing a deadly arc before her.

Wielding the blade with as much strength as she could, she slashed and jabbed the beast. Even trapped in a solid form, it made for a difficult target. Her blows reverberated, as if hitting stone. Her hand ached from the fierce grip she held on its hilt. Gritting her teeth against the sudden pain, she brought the sword around thrusting into the soft underbelly of the creature. It roared, raising its head to scream into the night and then charged toward her.

Stumbling, she caught herself; but the creature lashed out with claws sharper than any eagle's. She raised an arm to protect herself and felt the thing slash deep into her flesh....

Shade awoke, struggling frantically to free herself from what she soon realized was merely a tangle of damp bed sheets. As the silence of night huddled once more around her, she grew aware that her fists still clutched the crumpled bedding fearfully.

God, What a dream!

Even now it seemed the reek of the creature lingered in the airless room. Shade slowly released her grip on the bedding. Taking deep, slow breaths, she focused on the familiar landscape of her room. Her eyes followed the large Edward Gorey mural as it wrapped around the walls past candelabras, heavy velvet drapes, and her shelf full of voodoo dolls resembling various stars of reality TV.

Nothing seemed out of place. In fact, were it not for the lingering pall of fear and the sweat that now drenched her body, this night would have been like any other. Yet, she had trouble shaking the feeling that something was amiss.

Her legs felt damp, and she had a foolish thought that, had she switched on the light, she would have found them drenched in mud and gore. Craning her neck toward the nightstand, Shade read the glowing red numbers on the alarm clock: just a little after three in the morning.

It must have been that red-eye back from Salt Lake City, she thought. Shade didn't care much for flying, especially these days. It left her tense for hours afterward.

With a strange mixture of exhaustion and anxiety, she reluctantly pushed the blankets aside, crawled from bed, and slipped inside a pair of novelty slippers resembling large, hairy spiders. As she tightened her robe against the chill, Shade suddenly tensed.

The early morning quiet had been broken by a sudden scraping sound, which she sought desperately to identify. As the long, still moments passed, she was amazed at the sudden clarity of her perceptions. Like the figure in the dream, she stood poised for whatever waited in the night.

Shade moved cautiously toward the front rooms of the house. Moving slowly and daring not to breathe, she crept over the hardwood floors. Then she heard the sound again: a rapping followed by a screeching-scraping sound. Realizing what it was Shade shook her head ruefully.

That damn pine!

She glanced out the bank of windows, which wrapped around the front corner of her large Craftsman bungalow, to confirm the culprit: a wind-gnarled pine scraping against the glass with each gentle gust of wind. Shade was paying for her procrastination.

Got to remember to trim that thing.

She decided it had been the claw-like scratching of that branch that had invaded her dreams, manifesting itself as some horrid beast.

To be sure, Shade checked the lock on the door. It was solid; but still, she remained uneasy.

Shade peered into the dark Colorado morning, her eyes traveling across Beltline and up the gentle slope of Boulder Mountain Park before coming to rest on the familiar, jagged edges of the Flat Irons. The lights of the city illuminated peculiar, gangrenous clouds that sank low, nearly obscuring the iconic peaks.

Strange color, she thought with an uneasy sense of portent. Tugging the belt tighter, she winced in sudden pain. Slashed across the back of her hand, were several raw abrasions exactly where the creature had scratched her in the dream. What was going on? Her psychic dreams had never before affected her waking reality.

I probably just scratched myself while I was asleep.

She didn't fully buy that explanation.

No stranger to dreams, Shade knew this was what she feared most: a frightening dream with the strange, familiar feel of portent. She had her share of prophetic dreams from time to time, but they were often vague and occluded.

However, this vision was resolved and absolute. The woman in her dream had been Shade and Shade had been the woman. The creature had slashed at a stranger, but Shade now possessed the physical reality of it. What's more, the scratches were carved into the same hand the woman in the dream used to defect the beast's deadly blow.

    She did not yet know what it all meant but one thing was certain—it would not be good.

5

Sitting in her usual parking space in front of the Corvus Mound Archaeological Center, Dr. Karen Houston fingered the back of her hand. It was the same spot where the sword-wielding Amazon in her dream had blocked the creature's sharp claws.

No physical indications that it had been real; yet it had seemed so vivid, she half expected to find those same slashes cut into her own flesh. Oddest of all, it burned. Less now, to be sure, but earlier she had awakened to the very real pain of an abraded hand. She even thought it looked a little red. In fact, she was sure it was.

She couldn't understand it and this left her unnerved. Karen had always prided herself on having a knack for deciphering sense from even her murkiest dreams, but this....

"It was only a dream," she repeated aloud, knowing it was fast becoming a mantra against the unrest she felt. She had planned to get an early start on the Ennis Mound, but now she was strangely reluctant to even enter the building until the rest of the staff arrived.

Karen caught a glimpse of herself in her rearview mirror: bleary eyes punctuated an otherwise fresh face. Inwardly, she simply shrugged and pulled her hair back into a ponytail. Karen would be the first to admit she was a low-maintenance woman who scarcely wore makeup. Her girl-next-door looks allowed her to pull off such a feat.

The Get-Kwik just down the road was open, she thought to herself. *I'll get some coffee and be like new.*

She had just reached for the key in the ignition when the cold, metallic feel instantly recalled the sword the woman had wielded so ferociously in the dream.

She wondered if the nightmare had been a manifestation of her own anxieties. Professionally, Karen had come to Corvus Mound to further excavate the ancient hillocks constructed by the region's Caddoan predecessors. It was a subject both passionate and personal. She had grown up in the area and this early fascination led her to archaeology.

Truthfully, Karen would have to admit, Steve Hewitt *had* to be a major contributing factor to any nightmare.

Maybe he was the monster in my dream, she thought.

It made sense. How she had ever thought the man was in any manner attractive or appealing, Karen would never know. Unfortunately she had, and the result had been a disastrous affair. Steve had been her doctoral advisor, which was scandalous enough, but when one factored in his marriage, two kids, and the fifteen year age gap....

After a while, his promises of divorce began falling on deaf ears. Imagine sleeping with him and then learning he was married with two children. She cringed, remembering the feel of his damp lips on her even after all this time. She felt positively ill at the thought of anything more. Well, it was clear to Karen that she needed to get away.

When this job became available, it seemed perfect. Karen had many pleasant memories of Corvus Mound. Childhood trips into the "big town" with her aunt were always filled with little adventures and a treat or two. It was here, away from the University, that Karen felt both her professional and private lives could heal.

A few short minutes later, Karen was seated in a corner booth in the Get-Kwik's ad hoc café. After ordering a cup of coffee, she opened her valise and pulled out a sheaf of photocopies.

Personal issues aside, Karen's true passion was not a man, but a subject. She had been almost driven to learn about early cultures. Her studies into history had been a siren call, leading her ever further into human past. Sometimes it seemed she was seeking answers to questions she could not even begin to articulate, as if intuition guided her.

Her undergraduate studies were fraught with uncertainty. She had been unsure of her major for a few years, simply taking the classes that drew her interest: history, archaeology, and literature. Where people came from and how they arrived were the questions that intrigued her most. Seemingly obsessed, Karen had studied the mythology, language, and art of ancient cultures across the globe. As a result, there was a large block of course work dealing with the most ancient aspects of human history.

Eventually advisors began to urge her toward archaeology and she never looked back. In retrospect, she could never understand how her path had been anything but clear. During her coursework, she began seeing unusual connections and tantalizing clues to something more.

The Corvus Mounds were exciting: a site created by people nearly a thousand years removed—perhaps more. Not much was known about them and they were usually only referred to by the generic term, Moundbuilders. Karen, however, had her own theories.

She saw the strong Mesoamerican connections. There was a striking resemblance between ceremonial mounds and the temples of the Maya and Aztec. She saw their influence in Moundbuilder art and pottery. Moreover, she saw few connections to North American tribes of the period. It all begged the question: where did they really come from and why, such a short time later, did they seem to simply vanish?

Exactly who the earliest groups were was still a highly controversial subject.

The Corvus Mounds were not as well known as sites in Illinois, Snake Mound in Ohio, or the mounds of Mississippi and Georgia. They weren't even as recognized as their own sister site, just a few miles away at Spiro. But they were far more compelling.

Unfortunately, archaeology is a field strewn with volatile land mines of both dogma and political correctness, making any challenge to accepted theories professionally hazardous. More than once Karen had found herself alienated by the academic community for her *Diffusionist* views.

How she detested that word, especially when it was hurled like an epithet at her from other scientists.

To Karen, the Diffusionists were crackpots who grasped at every tenuous thread as validation that invariably ancient Atlanteans (or worse—aliens) were the earliest visitors to the New World. It was, they often argued, the only way the ignorant, backward natives of the Americas could ever have accomplished works such as the great pyramids at Tikal or Tenochtitlán. Karen found that sort of pseudo-science, championed by untrained armchair archaeologists, to be tabloid at best, making the insult all the more demeaning.

The tingling in her hand began once more just as the bell over the café door jingled and a handsome young man entered. Glancing from the stranger back to her hand, Karen noticed five red welts slashed across its back. *That's weird*, she thought. *Maybe I had an allergic reaction to that new lotion.*

Those thoughts were quickly pushed aside, however, when she better glimpsed the new arrival. Strangers in small towns are always a point of interest, but when they are also well dressed and attractive they become magnets, drawing every eye.

The man, who Karen figured to be about thirty, held her gaze briefly in his dark eyes before deciding upon a table near the front windows. Blushing a little, Karen found herself admiring the man at her periphery. He was tall, nicely built, and wore his shock of chestnut hair with casual indifference. His color was the sort of natural tan that Karen had always envied but a long line of pasty Scottish ancestors made difficult to achieve.

Seemingly oblivious to the attention he was generating, the stranger spent a lot of time looking across the road to the river where it cut across Henry Thompson's land. Karen noticed the welts had vanished once more.

At a nearby table, Karen heard the words "Montford Arms Hotel" and blatantly eavesdropped.

"No, what about it?" a woman was saying between bites of her breakfast.

"It's official. They're planning an opening gala in a few weeks," a man's voice replied. "There's an article in *The Oklahoman*. There will be a big press conference today, right here in town."

"That's fast! I thought there was still a bit of work to do."

"Well, it says here that when the hotel reopens, it will be in a limited capacity at first. That historic renovation company from Chicago will keep working even after guests arrive."

Karen thought over what she knew about the Montford Arms. The abandoned hotel, which still sat hoary but proud atop the hill, comprising much of old downtown Corvus Mound, was once considered the seat of the Donaldson empire.

The Donaldsons were early Oklahoma entrepreneurs with Midas-like hands in oil, politics, mining, and real estate. After some legal haggling, the family once again owned the hotel and now rumor had it that young Rick Donaldson had big plans for the place.

For several months now, the hotel had been under quiet renovation. Donaldson's sudden interest in the community where his family had once lived seemed a strong sign of a promising future many wanted to believe in.

"I still don't get who would come out here to stay in a hotel," the woman continued. "There's nothing out here but some old mounds and abandoned coal mines."

"Maybe there are other plans. Just think of the condos you could create there…"

"I've seen farther commutes, anyway."

"Oh, get this!" He began reading aloud. "There are some who claim that the Montford Arms is haunted."

"Give me a break! You and my landlady would get along just fine. She's crazy, too."

"No, really. Listen to this: 'the new owner is considering a scientifically-based examination of the hotel. He said that whatever they might discover could only add to the colorful history of this grand old establishment.' Sheesh! Talk about purple prose!"

"Who was it that said a sucker's born every minute? I smell a big publicity stunt. Watch, I bet you anything it ends up profiled on the Travel Channel with an obnoxious narrator who heaps new abuse on old puns."

The man, affecting an accent that Karen found to be a surprisingly dead-on imitation of a *Ghostly Travels* narrator, added: "The vacancy sign is never off at this hotel!"

The two laughed uproariously for a moment until the woman glanced at her wrist, noted she was late for work, and made a hurried exit.

Karen mulled over the conversation she just heard. She loved it when people appreciated the value of historic buildings. It had become so commonplace to raze old structures that Karen was grateful when anything was spared the wrecking ball.

The idea that the hotel was haunted made her wonder what else she could find about the Montford Arms in the museum's Historical Society records. *Might be fun to do a special display to mark the re-opening of the hotel.* Karen made a note to mention it to Paul Goodwin, the chief curator and her fellow Site Administrator.

In addition to being a permanent study site for the University of Oklahoma, and its affiliated

Museum of Natural History, The Corvus Mounds Archaeological Center also housed its own small museum, covering the region's natural history and historical records.

Under the previous administration, visitors were few and far between—school trips, mostly—but these days more visitors were discovering the Center, thanks in large part to Karen's efforts. And of course, there was the regular crowd of retirees who practically lived in their genealogy library.

This hotel business could boost some revenue for the mounds, especially if the town were going to start seeing more tourists. She had to speak to Paul and quickly. It looked like the Center could hitch its wagon to Mr. Donaldson's star.

6

The Corvus Mound Archaeological Center occupied eighty two acres just east of downtown, along the Arkansas River. The Center and its accompanying museum were housed in several discreet, aesthetically barren buildings, which had apparently passed for architecture in the early seventies.

The only thing Karen Houston found remotely attractive about her new digs was the black marble floor, which filled the museum's main gallery. It was one of the few things left undamaged when a large fire devoured much of the old First National Bank in downtown Corvus Mound—a bank made famous by having been victim to one of Pretty Boy Floyd's famous withdrawals.

Now, the tile dully reflected glass cabinets filled with fading signs recounting the region's history from Precambrian trilobites to pre-Columbian nomads, the Mound Builders, and on through the short-lived coal industry, oil boom, and subsequent decades of decline.

As Karen walked straight through the hall, passing smaller galleries filled with more natural history, art, and cultural artifacts, she could not help but feel a sense of pride at what she had accomplished here in her short tenure.

When she had first arrived, the site was run by a stodgy old curator named Buster Roberts who viewed the whole post as a way-station on the road to retirement. Not satisfied with merely replacing Roberts as caretaker, Karen had quickly begun turning things around. She hired graduate students for summer excavations, wrote endless grants for funding, and fast-tracked the preservation of countless artifacts long-trapped in storage rooms onsite. She was also instrumental in setting up an on-loan exhibit of items the Oklahoma Natural History Museum kept in storage. Karen even managed to gather a small staff of volunteer docents and the old, never-needed boardroom now held lectures and monthly presentations by local groups.

Karen was also very proud of establishing a partnership with the County Historical Library to lease the Center's large suite of equally needless executive offices to house its genealogy library. Now on any given day, retirees and young mothers could be seen poring over microfilm readers and old family histories, searching for their roots.

Karen Houston had taken over a sleepy, under-funded site and turned it into a world class facility. *Well, at least a popular stop for elementary schools*, she thought with a smidgen of mirth.

As Karen passed through the double doors, which separated the main museum from the offices and labs in the back, she waved at Marie Spelling, the County Historian, sitting at her desk. After nearly two years working in the museum, Karen was finally beginning to feel at home.

There were now currently five full-time employees of the Museum, three with the Historical Society and, including Karen, two archaeologists from the University of Oklahoma—not to mention the dozen undergraduate and graduate students who had begun to show up already. It was a small, closely-knit group that had finally begun to feel something like a family.

The hub of activity was the office Karen shared with the other site administrator, Paul Goodwin. It was cramped—only fifteen feet by twelve feet—but home. A home filled with tall metal storage shelves. Desks sat in each corner, lit only by small, barred windows and banks of fluorescent lighting. The whole room had a penal air about it.

Karen's own space was crowded with half-finished paperwork and a few of the prized artifacts exhumed from the mounds, awaiting preservation. The only item not related to her work was a colorful poster of Monet's Water Lilies, which had only been hung to cover a crack in one wall.

Karen was taking multitasking to the limit. Not only did she supervise excavation of the mounds, but she did a lot of digging herself on top of other curatorial duties, administrative tasks, grant writing and keeping up with her requirement to publish regularly. Anyone else would be on a fast-track to burnout but Karen loved it too much.

Around noon, Marie poked her head in Karen's door. "It's Mexican at the diner today. A bunch of us are heading over for some enchiladas and heartburn. Wanna come?"

"Small towns can look boring on the surface, but..." Marie paused, waiting for the waitress to leave, before she continued in a conspiratorial whisper. "Believe me, there is usually a lot of stuff that goes unnoticed."

"Like what?" Karen asked salaciously.

"Take your mounds, for instance. Did you know that there were some miners that disappeared around there in the early part of the last century? Rumor was they had been hired to loot the site."

"Pot hunters!" Karen grunted in disgust.

"They worked for O'Malley Mining, the company Silas Montford bought out before he built the hotel."

"You know, a similar thing happened at Spiro," Karen added. "Treasure hunters almost destroyed Craig Mound with their digging, ruining those artifacts they didn't loot. Mummified remains were even thrown aside and left to rot in the elements. We still know so little, any loss is a tragedy."

Karen's lament was shattered by the enticing aroma of cheap diner enchiladas. As the two began to eagerly consume their meals, conversation shifted to other topics.

She never saw the elderly man at the nearby table eavesdropping, a thoughtful look etched upon his weathered brown face. As he stood to leave the diner, he paused long enough to take one more look at the young woman sitting at the table. He wanted to be able to recognize her again.

7

Mr. Spencer! Mr. Spencer!" Camera flashes machine-gunned the car as it drew to a smooth stop in front of the Montford Arms Hotel.

Good, Marshall Spencer thought in satisfaction. *All the major news outlets are here. Everything is on track.*

For too long Spencer had been little more than a paper-pusher when it came to filing annual property taxes and other fees associated with the languishing old hotel. Now that Donaldson was in full ownership, Spencer saw his opportunity to rise from the muck. He assumed quickly the role of Donaldson's in-state spokesperson and was already leveraging this high profile status into greater opportunities. Maybe even a run at some type of office.

His mood darkened as he saw a tall, familiar blonde plunging through the crowd, dragging her cameraman on a short leash. She patted her hair, tidying non-existent strands.

Great. Channel 6 sent Skyler Dunworth-Michaels.

Spencer gave himself a quick glance in the visor mirror before exiting the large sedan. He strode over to the barricaded entrance where a massive chain and padlock rested incongruously across a pair of delicate art nouveau doors of bronze and glass. Spencer stepped to one side, inspecting a large plaque set in the granite foundation. As if unaware of the milling crowd, he lovingly traced the words "Montford Arms."

That's sure to make the cut for the evening news—probably with a voice over by one of these obnoxious bottom dwellers pontificating on the firm's commitment to preserving history.

He turned to address the small crowd, "My client wishes to announce his plans: The Montford Arms Hotel will have its grand opening July Fourth weekend. There will be a black tie gala, tours, musical concerts, and special grand opening rates! This will bring much needed economic growth, and more importantly, new jobs to this corner of the state!"

As he had expected, there were some loud cheers from pedestrians passing by who had stopped to watch. In fact, he had planned it just the day before; knowing how well it would it would play on camera.

"Rick Donaldson's decision," he continued thunderously, "to use mostly local labor has meant over four hundred jobs for Corvus Mound."

More cheers erupted from the crowd and Spencer soaked it all in like the warm caress of a sunny day.

A shadow fell over his revelry as he spied Skyler Dunworth-Michaels shoving her way through the cluster of reporters, wetting her crimson lips like some vicious jungle cat. She thrust a microphone into Spencer's face.

"Congratulations on such a long-deserved accomplishment! What are your plans now?" she called out, and without waiting for an answer, "Have you been retained by Donaldson for any other projects? Are you considering a run for governor?"

Staggering under the reporter's non-sequiturs, Spencer could only hold up his hands, "My plans are not really important right now. What is important is that this will open wide the door to economic expansion and development in our part of the state. It is a positive move that will benefit everyone."

"Thank you for coming, folks." Waving to the cluster of people, he tossed a final smile on the reporters. "No further questions!" He saluted the crowd and ducked back into the waiting limo.

Turning away sharply, Skyler elbowed her way back through the crowd cursing under her breath, "Bastard! Self-important—Move it, Scott!"

Later that afternoon, Skyler stepped into Harold Mason's office as he was on the phone.

"Skyler, I'm on an important call here…." The segment producer began.

A long, well-manicured nail tapped the framed photograph of a mousy Mrs. Mason and a smiling pack of little Harold clones. She saw the characteristic blush rise from his neck and spread onto his face. One slip over a year ago still had him worried about his wife finding out.

"Hey, something has come up here," he told the caller. "Can I call you back?"

Skyler was furious enough to chew nails—or station managers. Especially those slimy office clowns who didn't know a good story from a steaming pile of crap. Since the fiasco with Spencer out in Corvus Mound that morning, the day had gone quickly to hell. The van had a flat on the way back to Tulsa, she was late for another interview, and now Harold Mason had the balls to pull this shit.

"Good morning, Skyler. Is there a problem?"

"You know what the problem is!" She tossed the memo onto the mostly empty desk. "Where did this come from? Why am I being pulled off of a story that is, by all rights, mine!"

"Please!" He got up and closed the office door with a fearful look on his gaunt face. "This is not my call. I am just the go-between. This comes from the station manager, in fact."

"You gave my story to Jamison? You knew that I was trailing Spencer. I've been tracking his legacy of corruption for months now."

"Others were doing the same thing. You hardly exist in a vacuum."

"I've done all the leg work on his background, I learned about the bar association bribes, and I was the one who was tipped on his plans to run for governor."

"All of which means nothing."

"I hunted down both his ex-wives and a string of girlfriends to get exclusives no one else could touch. You knew all of this and you still took it!"

"The station maintains the prerogative."

"You can't expect me to drop a story like that and do this...this...*fluff piece* on a damned hotel in the middle of nowhere!"

"The manager wants you on it. End of story."

"You've got to be kidding! You expect me to do some bullshit Scooby Doo filler?"

"Ghosts are big ratings these days. So, he wants you to get one of these teams like the ones on TV and follow them around."

"It's career suicide and you know it. Who will take me seriously as a journalist with something like this? It's not news! It's not even in the City or Tulsa. It's in a dusty country town where they roll up the sidewalks at sunset."

"It'll be fine."

"It-is-my-story!" She ground out.

"Skyler…."

"I am an award-winning television journalist, known for always getting what I set out to get. I always get the story. Maybe there is another story here that needs to be explored, hmm? Corruption in the newsroom? How a few well-placed bribes might get a stogy station manager to put somebody else on a story to protect the interests of an old friend?"

"He's already decided, Skyler." Mason shuffled several stacks of paper meaninglessly. "My hands are tied. We're through here now. Go hand your film from this morning over to Jamison."

Striding down the hallway, Skyler continued to fume.

This isn't over, she thought. *I have some connections of my own, after all. Plenty of options available. Maybe it was time I explored my horizons.* She remembered her interview with that Donaldson character. *He seemed to be making an enticing offer....*

But first, she would take up teaching. The lesson to be learned: don't mess with Skyler Dunworth-Michaels and expect to get away with it.

8

In trench CM-5 at Ennis Mound—one of the many smaller ones that had been spared looters eighty years before—Karen carefully brushed loose soil from the clay pot, revealing details of a shaman effigy. After taking a series of shots *in-situ* with her camera, Karen worked carefully to remove the vessel from the surrounding matrix.

Unlike the meticulously painted wares of the southwest cultures, the Moundbuilders formed simpler vessels with little ornamentation. Among the few exceptions were the artfully-wrought effigies resembling deities from the native pantheon: turtles, frogs, and various birds. Wrapping around the jar she now held in her hands was an effigy fashioned to resemble a holy man holding up a smaller vessel.

Karen admired these pieces the most. They were compelling evidence for her argument of a strong Mesoamerican influence on the Mississippian culture–not arising from trade or proximity, though. Karen's theory was that an older culture influenced both.

As she excavated the mounds, she kept finding vague but tantalizing clues that something was missing; an important piece of the puzzle was gone. There were also indications that a larger mound had once existed in service to some kind of death cult. Karen felt certain that if she could find and excavate the remains of a lost mound, she would have her answers.

She quickly finished jotting down measurements in her field book and then placed the vessel carefully into a carton for further lab work. As she turned back to replace the marker flag that would designate the exact spot from which the pot was removed, a dull glint caught her eye. Grabbing a soft brush, Karen began gently removing the loose soil from where the pot once sat.

"This has got to be some kind of joke!" Karen stared for several long moments in astonishment at the artifact she had just revealed.

It was unmistakably a sword—perhaps two and a half feet long—with an intricately carved golden hilt and a vague sense of familiarity about it. The blade widened along the center in a style similar to the Harrappa or even the Akkadians, cultures that predated the Babylonians and may have been among the first to populate the lands between the Tigris and Euphrates rivers.

Site contamination? She wondered. *God knows those pot hunters weren't the most careful lot. A joke? Reynolds! I bet it was Reynolds. He's been teasing me about my fascination with....*

Even as she rationalized, Karen knew it was none of those scenarios. This particular mound had never been excavated, and Reynolds was too professional to risk site contamination for a few laughs.

The gilded sword before her was very real and very disturbing; no such weapon was known to the Moundbuilders. Even a cursory glance told her its style and construction was unlike anything in the New World.

A shudder of panic coursed through her for a brief moment. Contamination could call into question everything they had worked for at Corvus Mound. Karen quickly photographed, mapped, and annotated the find before removing the sword. She would need to keep a tight lid on this until she could get in touch with Dr. Wellston, the project head and chief curator of archaeology, at the University museum.

Karen slipped quietly back into her office, grateful Goodwin was nowhere around. Unlocking the bottom drawer to her file cabinet, Karen pulled the canvas-wrapped sword from her bag and quickly sequestered the piece within the drawer. This site contamination threatened everything she was working for at Corvus Mound, or at least that is how she would play it with Dr. Wellston.

After the initial shock wore off, Karen had to admit she was more than a little thrilled. In her gut, she knew this could validate her theories. Check your enthusiasm, Karen, she told herself. This will probably just turn out to be some sick joke.

Attempting to put the situation on the back burner, Karen opened the envelope Marie had left on her desk prior to escaping for lunch. She found a collection of photos and clippings for Matt Wolf.

Sure, she thought to herself, *I could have had Marie run them over, but it might be a good opportunity to network—especially with someone who regularly communicated with Donaldson.*

Karen knew that more and more, private companies were funding archaeology. She allowed herself to daydream momentarily about a year-round staff, budget surpluses, and a new museum.

9

Matt headed toward the fourth floor to inspect a massive drywall project that had taken the crew far too long. As he neared the spot where the old lathe and plaster walls were being torn down, he saw the men clustered around one section.

"Hey boss!" Jake called as he caught sight of Matt.

Matt moved slowly toward the men, fearing they were yet again ogling some centerfold instead of working. These local guys were good, but they needed more prodding than Matt was accustomed to giving.

"Look at this, boss. Somebody stashed this old cash box in the wall." Jake pointed to an old rusty box layered with drywall dust. "Wonder if it's got any money in it?"

"Probably some kid's rock collection," Matt returned with a grin.

"Or some guy's porn!" Jake shot back, laughing at his own wit.

Matt simply shook his head as he inspected the old box: the lock was solid. He turned it over and examined the back hinges. Most manufacturers were so concerned about keeping the lock strong that they ignored the hinges. If he worked at it, he just might be able to....

"Ah, there we go," he said proudly as the lid popped open.

Both men groaned upon finding it held only an old tattered journal, its desiccated leather cover flaking away. Matt opened the tome gingerly and read the fading spidery script: *Margaret Loretta Whitney*.

"Well, riches elude us once again. I guess it's back to work, huh?" Jake shrugged as he turned and shuffled from the room.

Poor guy, Matt thought with a tinge of empathy. It seemed Jake was looking for something big to come his way. Not as shiftless as Matt's father, but he was a dreamer just the same.

Turning back to the journal in his hands, Matt took a seat on an upturned five-gallon bucket and carefully began turning the pages....

June 12, 1925

I am so proud of my Gerald. Manager already of such a fine and respectable hotel as the Montford Arms! The hotel is filled with potential, he tells me. I believe he means that several highly-placed gentlemen have begun taking him under their wings. I look forward to our life together and I know that we will have happy times as we build a family in this lovely home and in such a promising community....

Obviously, the diary began when this woman's husband had assumed management of the hotel.

July 30, 1925

The Governor held a ball here last night, and the gowns of the ladies were so lovely! Next week the Senator has reserved rooms for him and his son. I am in such a state! I must make certain I do my Gerald proud and do everything in my power to help him succeed. I just wish that he did not spend so much time with Judge Clayton Forbes. He appears to be a man of some success and has every appearance of refinement, yet I am never comfortable in his presence.

Matt hardly paid attention to the clock ticking the minutes into hours as he was absorbed deeper into Margaret's strange world.

October 30, 1925

The spirit of Hallowe'en has invaded! I know that sounds melodramatic, but the episode today can hardly be described any other way. One of the maids came running in, screaming that she had seen "death." When I questioned her, she pointed to the low wall in the garden. A line of six crows stared boldly back at us. She kept repeating "six is for death, six is for death." When I demanded an answer, she ran sobbing out of the hotel. The head housekeeper had joined us by that time and she said it was just an old rhyme about crows: "One is bad luck, two is good luck, three is health, four is wealth, five is sickness, and six is death...."

I looked outside and saw another one take his place to make seven. Surely, I thought, that would cancel the bad luck and calm the maid.

When I noted this, the housekeeper (a woman who I had, until now, found quite sober-minded) paled until I feared for her health and then crossed herself.

"God save us," she whispered. Then, as if nothing had happened, she turned and walked away.

Gerald laughed when I recounted this. He shrugged it off as a good fireside tale, and I soon found myself laughing with him. Still, for some reason, I simply cannot forget the look on her face.

10

"There's a ghost in the hotel, you know."

Matt had just placed the last promotional poster—an homage to the Roaring Twenties—into one of the glass display boxes flanking the hotel's grand entrance when the voice spoke.

"I'm sorry?" Matt asked, turning to see an elderly woman looking at the display with great interest.

"My mother saw it once."

"What did you say?"

"It's certainly a nice advertisement, dear," she replied, seemingly oblivious to his question. "You've captured the raw energy of the time. I always loved stories of those days. Everything was booming then. So alive! Dirtier, true—all that oil and coal—but so much was going on you could probably forgive the mess."

She was casually dressed in cotton pants, an almost garish floral top, and sporting a large canvas bag emblazoned with a large tree and the words *Corvus Mound Historical Society.*

"What was that you said about a ghost?" Matt asked, cramming the cabinet keys in his pocket and picking up an empty box from the sidewalk. "You say your Mother saw one? You mean here at the hotel?"

"Yes. She had been working here at the time. She saw one of the ghosts on the fourth floor. Scared her silly! She refused to work those rooms ever again. Said it was the most frightening experience she ever had in her life."

"Your mother saw a ghost while she worked here?"

"Well, yes dear. Weren't you listening, young man?" The woman seemed a little annoyed that Matt was having so much trouble comprehending such a simple concept. "Now understand, Mama wasn't fanciful at all either. Why, she'd lived through the Depression, you know—and had seven kids. Fanciful she wasn't."

"And on the fourth floor...." Matt repeated, remembering something one of the workers had said earlier in the week. "Tell me, Mrs...."

"Bell. Rose Bell."

"Tell me, Mrs. Bell. What did your mother see, exactly?"

11

"Damn job!"

Chuck Bean had just finished his last job of the day, and was prepared to grab a beer over at Marty's, when his boss commanded him to look for some missing well over at the hotel.

As the one and only official field inspector for Corvus Mound, examining time wasters like this had fallen to him. Building a new garage? Old Chuck hauls ass over, inspects it, and slaps down a sticker saying it's okay to begin. Adding a driveway? Chuck will stop by and see you keep it all nice and legal. Find an old, damn smelly well, and Chuck is the one to climb down, take samples, and whatever the hell else was needed.

Damn job.

He might have postponed it until next week, using the holiday as an excuse. But he and Frank Sattler had never been buddies; the sooner he could get this done and away from the old coot, the better he'd feel. *Rip the bandage off*, he thought.

Chuck walked through a large service entrance off the back alley and into a large industrial kitchen. His boss had said Sattler wanted the old well checked out before the day was through. '*Trouble is…we don't know exactly where it is*,' Chuck smiled, recalling Sattler's sheepish admission.

"What a bunch of dumbfucks," Chuck grumbled as he turned down one of the halls in the old kitchen wing. As usual, it was up to him to bail someone's ass out of a sling.

He switched on the bulb dangling down the center from a thick black cord. Even in the wan light, the space seemed a little off to Chuck. Something wasn't right; he was sure of it. The size inside didn't quite match where he knew the adjoining wall should stand, for one thing. And while they were each painted the same institutional gray, one wall was definitely made from newer materials.

This has to be it, Chuck thought. This has got to be the well. Must have closed it up after they got city water back in the twenties?

Chuck continued surveying the room without much excitement for the task ahead. He remembered when old lady Kramer had him over to find her well. "It's over here," she had whined. "I am sure of it." Minutes later he was up to his armpits in decades old crap. The old woman had led him straight to a forgotten septic tank.

Chuck yanked out his tape measure, determined to get this over with. Minutes later, glancing at his blueprints, Chuck knew without a doubt that Sattler was right. The plans showed a bigger room than this. A little over five feet at the far end was missing.

Wasted a lot of space, though, just closing off an end like that. But what do I care?

Tentatively, Chuck began tapping the wall, searching for studs and listening for voids.

Money hungry desk jockey's who never can keep their fingers out of people's pockets....

Within minutes he had the wall open and was breaking through the old batten and plaster.

Laws, rules, regulations....

It was an angry refrain building in his head, and with each word, his hammer went through the wall with more ferocity until a dark hole opened up. As Chuck leaned in with a flashlight, he saw the lip of an old well. A piece of wood served as a makeshift lid. Well, look at this. They closed it up behind a damned wall, for pity's sake. How much "safer" could that be?

A small, cool puff of air surged up from below. It smelled dry and dusty, not at all the dankness he expected.

That's strange, Chuck thought, *maybe the well dried up years ago*. Hefting himself through the hole, he shoved the lid out of the way, and took a closer look. It took him a minute or two before he realized this hole wasn't like any well he had seen before.

As he played his flashlight along the bottom, the beam danced over several white rocks. For a minute or two, he simply stared at the pile of stones, their shapes tantalizing his mind with elusive familiarity. Yet, even as recognition crept slowly forward, his mind refused to accept the reality of what he was seeing. Littering the bottom of the well were several skulls, as well as long bones and countless smaller remnants of the human form. The flashlight in his hand trembled as he counted more than half a dozen skulls within the mass grave.

A faint and indescribable sound caught his attention from the dark shadows of the opening, just beyond his light. With each tremulous breath, the sound grew louder. Playing the light along the bottom, Chuck tried in vain to pinpoint its source but as he leaned in closer, the flashlight slipped from his hand.

"Damn!"

The light spun cartwheels around the room as Chuck desperately tried to seize it, but his feet lost purchase on the well's loose stone rim. His arms wind-milled for a few seconds as he attempted to steady himself but it was useless. In an instant, Chuck plunged to the ground ten feet below.

"Damn! Damn! Damn!"

Chuck coughed hard and spat dirt from his mouth. It took him a moment to shake his head clear and realize he now lay sprawled among the bones. Quickly scrambling on his haunches, he scooted away from the macabre sight. As he did, a shower of tiny stones, loosened by his fall, cascaded from the walls above, enveloping him in a fresh haze of dust.

Checking himself out, he sat up slowly with a wheezing cough. He tried in vain to wave the dust away but the dust cloud only reformed.

At least nothing's broken, he thought morosely.

Chuck rested his back against the stone wall as he tried to regain his breath. In the stillness that followed, he noticed the sound he had first heard moments before was now much louder. The resonance was like the hiss of steam or the drone of insects. Chuck picked up the flashlight and probed the well around him.

"What the hell is that?"

The light wavered, and then flickered. Chuck smacked it a few times and the beam shone brightly once more. He played the light across the surface of the well, searching for what had caught his eye. To Chuck's left, a strange slab sat embedded in one of the earthen walls.

Flapping away the lingering dust, he peered closer. The fissured stone was roughly four feet high with cryptic symbols scrawled across its surface.

Thinking it might have some value, Chuck decided to swipe a piece of it. *I bet old Bob Raines down at the jewelry store will know what this thing's worth*, he thought with anticipation. Chuck allowed himself to daydream for just a moment. If this was some ancient Indian artifact, then it could be just the thing to get him out from under his debts. The amount of money he owed the bank had been piling up steadily since he foolishly took out that second mortgage to pay for his daughter's wedding.

After tugging at one of the looser fragments with his hands proved fruitless, Chuck pulled out a screwdriver and began wedging it into the seams of rock. The humming suddenly intensified and Chuck felt something push against the slab. The force was strong like the onrush of water and he was knocked roughly back against the ground.

Without even time to recover, Chuck felt himself suddenly being churned around within the confines of the well like laundry. He was trapped in a roiling embrace of Motion and sound. A foul, metallic taste, like blood, filled his mouth as the soft hum grew into a roar that assaulted every inch of his body. Chuck managed to gain a moment of purchase and staggered to his feet. Swaying a bit as he stumbled toward the wall, Chuck felt the world tilt as his face paled and he retched violently onto the dank floor.

Grabbing the stones in places where the mortar had long since eroded, Chuck forced himself up and away from the pit.

Gotta get away...gotta get out of here....

Only inches from the top, Chuck's strength quickly drained from his trembling arms. Too busy marshalling his remaining strength to make it over the rim, Chuck couldn't see that something was now snaking about within the shadows at the bottom of the well.

An inky tendril of smoke probed the pit, seeking its prey.

It struck!

Grabbing Chuck's leg, the thing sunk into his flesh, and began dragging him into the depths. The inspector's panicked cries were lost within a roaring hum that filled his brain with heat and pain, choking off all but the most primal of thoughts.

Gotta get out of here! Chuck clung with desperation to the rim of the well, heavy beads of sweat clustering on his face. Blood covered his hands as he clawed frantically at the sharp outcroppings of rock.

With the exhilaration of hope, Chuck heard the construction crew in the distance. With one last heave, he managed to pull himself out of the hole, crashing heavily to the floor. Wiping his face, Chuck left a bloody smear across his forehead, but it did not matter—he was alive. He staggered to his feet, feeling the dizziness wash over him again.

"Oh crap," he muttered as bile rose sourly. An instant later, he retched fiercely onto the cement floor. Chuck had only one thought as he wiped the sick from his face.

Damn job!

12

Skyler slipped from the bed carefully to avoid waking the man beside her. There was a certain reluctance to leave, remembering the previous night. The scent of his cologne still clung to the air around her. The aroma—*Creed*, she thought—telegraphed not only money, but a classic elegance she found lacking in most men. He was so unlike the other men she dated: cultured, successful, and almost impossibly handsome. It was a trifecta few women would encounter, fewer still could resist.

"Hmmm…." A groggy grumbling halted her departure. "Where are you going? Come back to bed." One tanned arm reached out to grab at her as she stood up. Then it dropped limply back to the bed as he grumbled into the pillow that it was too early to get up.

"You stay there," Skyler responded as she tucked the arm back under the sheets. "I have to catch an early flight, remember? Go back to sleep."

Even as he mumbled a response, she sensed he was already asleep. *True,* Skyler thought, *Rick Donaldson may be a lethal combination for any woman, but he wasn't without his shortcomings, either.* She knew, in the cruel light of day, his self-absorption and single-minded quest to rise to the top made him ill-suited for the role of paramour.

Yet, it was these very aspects of his personality that she had counted on to get her idea launched and, more importantly, funded. Lucky for her, his interests extended from spreadsheets to bed sheets.

Normally, she would have been getting up at the crack of dawn to get to the studio for the early news broadcast. Oh, how she hated dragging herself out of a nice warm bed every morning. She had been stuck in that time slot for a couple of years without anything happening to move her out that rut. A nice evening anchor slot was what she deserved and what she would get.

Now, this latest piece of business. Damned if she was going to let those bastards ruin her! Imagine tossing that idiotic story into her lap as she was leaving for the evening. She would be a laughing stock with serious journalists and lose any hopes of moving up and out.

A sudden vision of being trapped at the station for eternity had her clenching her jaw just to restrain the urge to scream. Especially since her mother had called to say that her sister just finished another article for Newsweek. Ultimately, Skyler had to admit that was why she had ended up in Donaldson's apartment last night. She had realized his potential for helping her, if he was properly motivated.

Dragging a brush through her hair, Skyler vowed to herself that she would make her own future. From now on she was instigating the kill rather than simply waiting for the scraps tossed to her by brainless twits like Jameson.

Donaldson was still just a lump under the sheets a few minutes later as she left the apartment. She knew from her research into the business tycoon that it was unlikely he would wake anytime before noon.

She paused in the hallway to make sure that the check he had given her was still there. She could get used to seeing that many zeros on a check with her name. She would do their story on the haunted history of the old Montford Arms hotel, all right. But she was going to do it her way.

They might be plotting to obliterate her, but she would survive. There was big money these days in "reality" ghost programs. If she hired her own crew....

She was impatient now that she had a plan and the financing.

As she hailed a taxi back to the airport, Skyler mentally assembled a list of people she needed to contact. Things were moving quickly now in a direction that posed a whole new set of possibilities for the future. It was a new game and this time she would come out the winner.

13

The screen door squealed harshly as it slammed shut. Matt Wolf walked across the creaking boards of the back porch to where his grandfather sat rocking in an old cane-backed chair.

"I'll have to oil that again," he said. "Before I head back to Corvus, I'll take care of it. All this spring rain must have rusted it out again."

His grandfather simply nodded silently.

He had oiled it a million times over the years, but today the chore was an annoyance. Matt realized it was something that bothered him far more than it should have. There was a tension in the air that had him unaccountably jumpy.

Standing by the door, Matt studied the old man for a moment: a long mane of gray hair was tied behind him with a leather lace. A lifetime of responsibility had carved deep ravines into his aged countenance. But there was also a weariness to his eyes, something new that gave Matt a chill of fear. A sense of resignation had washed over the old man since Matt's last visit.

Maybe it was time to take him into Corvus or to one of those assisted living places in Tulsa that his cousin, Molly, was always talking about.

Matt followed the old man's gaze as stared out across the tree-blanketed hills, a peaceful enough place most of the time. Growing up, it had been a solace to him as he struggled to find his identity in an amazingly complex world. But it was also a world filled with painful memories.

Matt unconsciously traced a path down his right cheek, the scar almost imperceptible these days, a souvenir of that fatal night. Seemed like most of his life his dad had been either drunk or in jail. As a child, he had often hated the man for denying him and his mother the life they should have had. The life they could have had if only his father had been stronger, braver, or just…*different*.

Not being Native American herself, Matt's mother would send him to his grandfather's for the summers to connect with his tribal roots. His grandfather told him impossible stories about his people and how someday he would be called upon to do something important. Matt didn't have time to listen to old medicine man nonsense. He was too eager to hike out over the far hills and put as much distance between him and his past as possible. As soon as he had graduated from high school, Matt went to the most distant college that would accept him.

A lot of water had flowed under the bridge since then. It all seemed like a lifetime ago—someone else's.

Matt felt the sweat trickle down his back. It was another hot Oklahoma day—and it wasn't even June yet. He hated days like this when the air hung moist and still.

Today especially.

There was a strange tension in the air, as if something were about to happen. Yet, nothing moved in the hazy sky or in the silent hills, dense with blackjack oak. Still, he found his eyes constantly seeking them out, watching for something.

Once, as a child, he had been walking with his parents along a dusty back road flanked on either side by thick forests aflame in autumnal colors. Overhead, a low ceiling of gray clouds seemed to hang just above the treetops. Matt had been pouting about something—he couldn't remember what—and dragged his feet protest, falling further and further behind his parents with each step. When he finally looked up from his sulking, he was surprised to find them gone. And it struck him how still things were. Gone was the murmur of his parent's conversation. Gone was the boisterous cackling of field birds. It seemed the light gray sky was descending lower, seeking him out. He had run like crazy to find his parents who scoffed at him and made light of the tears he fought.

Matt felt some of that day now as he watched the still landscape that seemed poised with anticipation.

As if reading his mind, a cluster of crows burst from of a thicket, darting out across the hillside. Their harsh cries rang like cathedral bells through the torpid air.

"Damn crows!" the old man muttered with surprising energy. "I always hated them."

"Sure are loud." Matt followed the eruption of black feathers as they rose into the sky. "Maybe there's a storm brewing. Where's that radio we got to monitor the weather?"

"Never mind that now, Matt!" His grandfather began, his tone conveying a sudden seriousness. "There's something you need to know, something I've been putting off your whole life."

Matt stared intently at his grandfather, a small knot of panic twisting in the pit of his stomach.

"Nothing ever happened in all this time," Ben Yellow Wolf continued. "I thought it was safe. I thought maybe it was a lie; an old man's nonsense, after all."

"Grandpa, you all right?" Matt rushed closer, fearing the old man might be having a stroke.

"I have failed my father and his father, too."

The crows returned, darting in and out of the brush.

"You're tired. Come on, let me get you inside."

The birds noisily fluttered their wings as they bunched together, almost conspiratorially, along the fence line. Their beady eyes seemed to glare back at the two men.

"How many crows are there?" the old man's voice demanded, suddenly full of some mysterious intensity.

"What?"

"How many?"

Matt searched his grandfather's face, looking for meaning. None. He turned his gaze once more to the crows. One, two, three....

"Looks like five.... No, make that six."

"Things are happening, Matt!" His grandfather never raised his voice, yet somehow it conveyed the sound of thunder rumbling in the distant hills.

"Maybe you need to go lie down on the bed for a while?" Matt began to pick Ben up, but met a firm resistance.

"I had hoped I would never have to tell anyone what my father told me, secrets his father had told him. Secrets that go all the way back, longer than memory—longer than these hills. Things are happening, though. Too many things, and I am afraid you need to know the truth."

"What truth?" Matt struggled to understand what his grandfather was trying to say. Has he lost his mind?

"The truth about who we are," Ben motioned for him to sit. "You have spent most of your life running away in anger from your family. And to be honest, we weren't always the best of families. Your father, for instance—"

"My father was a drunk!" Matt was surprised at the anger that seeped into that brief statement. After all these years, there was still so much vitriol.

"Matt, you don't understand what your father had to deal with."

"My father was a weak-willed drunk who left his family to suffer the consequences. That's what drinking did to him!"

"No, Matt," his grandfather countered softly. "That is what I did to him. I was the one who dragged him out to help me fight the evil when he wasn't ready—and I only half-believed the old tales myself. All we had to do was stand guard. Whenever the evil woke up, we performed the ritual."

"Come on, grandpa. You know I don't buy into any tribal medicine man crap!"

Ben Yellow Wolf ignored his grandson, "Only one thing to do and I messed that up. So, your father ended up paying the highest price for my mistake. You see, as a child, my own father was killed during the Second World War and I had been a poor pupil of his. I was a lot like you. I didn't believe anything he said about our purpose—and the hotel."

"The hotel?" Matt queried. A strange sense of foreboding began to stir.

"My father had fought the evil there before with the help of a local woman. Part of me really thought it was all some silly story. So, that's how I raised your father. I robbed him of meaning and purpose, leaving him an empty shell. It's no wonder he drank himself to death, Matt. I am to blame."

"There is no way you are responsible. Don't talk this way."

"Matt, there is only one way to convince you of what I say." He fished an object from his pocket and held open his hand for Matt to take it.

"I wish there was another, because this won't be easy."

It was a small flask, a miniature clay canteen that hung from a cord like a necklace. Matt took it into his hand, noting the glyph on its surface depicting a strange, hulking beast. Indecipherable scribbles snaked along the edges of the unusual vessel, which felt cold in his hands.

"I just hope," began the old man, "that it is not too late."

14

"Ray gonna be all right, Mr. Wolf?" one of the workers asked as the ambulance pulled away from the curb in front of the Montford Arms.

Matt turned to the silent cluster of men milling on the sidewalk. He noted a new level of defensiveness and anxiety in them. They expected him to come down hard for their carelessness in causing such an accident. Maybe fire a couple of them.

"It's a clean break," Matt assured the worker. "The paramedics said he shouldn't have any problems."

He hoped that was true. This was the third accident in as many days, not including the city inspector.

Matt kneaded his neck, as he felt a familiar rope of stress forming a noose around him.

"Anyone see what happened?"

"He was fine one minute," Jim, an electrician, said in a bewildered tone. "Then he ran up to check on a cord he'd forgotten. The next thing I know, he'd fallen."

"He never falls. He's like a cat!" Eddie spoke up defiantly. "Worked with him for four years and he's never fallen. It's this place. It's haunted like they've been saying!"

A few weeks ago, Eddie would have been mocked relentlessly for uttering such an idea. But now, after three major accidents and a string of irksome troubles, it just didn't seem as impossible. On top of this, tempers were flaring and not just from the heat, which had moved in and taken up residence a week ago. Misplaced tools had caused two guys to go at it in the kitchen last week.

There were also other…occurrences. Matt hadn't believed it when the men started coming to him; usually one at time, afraid the crew would find out. Nervously they shared stories of unexplained voices, seeing people that weren't there, or tools that strangely went missing only to turn up far from where they had been lost. One or two of the men had asked to work somewhere—anywhere—other than whatever floor they had been on.

None were trying to con him into more pay or less work. These were no-nonsense men accustomed to giving their all. They tucked into their work with energy and diligence, but the anxiety was there nonetheless because they didn't understand it. And it was mounting with each incident. Fear gave rise to a lot of nonsense and superstition.

"It *is* haunted," Aaron, one of the youngest on the crew, responded emphatically. "My grandma was telling me just last night that this place used to be a portal to hell or something."

"And she's a God-fearin' woman." Jim nodded his head in earnest agreement.

Matt wasn't sure how much longer he could count on these guys before they began cracking under the strain. Feeling another twisting spasm in his neck, Matt realized the first causality might be himself.

"Yeah, I talked to an old timer." Eddie said with quiet intensity, his voice barely above a hoarse whisper. "He said this place was haunted too. He said it should've been burned down a long time ago."

"Come on Eddie, that's a load of bull and you know it!" Sattler pushed through the group and positioned himself in the middle of the sidewalk.

"Ray screwed up," Sattler continued. "Now we just gotta be more careful. These things happen in our business."

"Sattler's right," Matt spoke up. "I'll go over to the hospital and make sure Ray's all right. Then we'll all meet up at the bar—first round's on me."

"That's how we handle it," Sattler instructed. "So shut your traps about this haunted bullshit!" His glance pinned Eddie meaningfully. "Now, we're not gettin' paid to stand out here workin' on our tans, so get back to work!"

The crew responded with an air of relief. Sattler was yelling at them and the world was normal again. Matt only wished it was that simple.

"Matt," the crew boss said softly.

"What's on your mind, Sattler?" Matt continued to watch as most of the men returned to their jobs. A few, however, lingered on the sidewalk, shoulders bunched with frustration. "I'd be the last to admit it, but there is something strange going on around here lately. Now you know I ain't been listening to Eddie, but I have been using my eyes. I've been working construction for nearly forty years. I gotta tell ya, I ain't seen nothin' as this job."

Matt looked at the grizzled old foreman with apprehension. Not him too.

"Odd things are happenin', Matt. No doubt about it. Despite what I said to the men, there was somethin' strange about Ray's accident."

"What?" Matt asked. "Are you suggesting somebody is trying to sabotage us?"

"All I'm saying is that somethin' is goin' on here. Stop and think for a minute: Ray was working in an area that had nothin' to trip over, no stairs, no ladders, nothin' anywhere around him. He goes to fetch a length of cord and he falls and breaks a leg?"

"Maybe the cord got tangled in his feet?"

"It was still coiled together." Sattler glared at the hotel. "Explain that one to me."

This site was breaking all the rules, no doubt. Reluctantly, Matt was coming to agree that something about this place was jinxed.

He didn't have much time to ruminate on the mystery before a worker suddenly burst from the cluster of men to charge at him with a guttural roar.

"No!" Eddie screamed as he rammed into Matt, knocking him to the sidewalk. "You killed him! You'll kill us all!"

Once down, Eddie seemed intent on keeping him there. Matt was more concerned about protecting vital body parts from steel toed boots than returning blows.

"What the hell?" Sattler shouted. "Get off him!"

"You'll pay! You'll die!" Eddie's words made no sense.

"Eddie! Eddie, stop!" Matt coughed while dodging kicks.

Sattler rushed forward, but the younger man put him down with one blow, leaving him sprawled on the pavement.

Matt's inattention won him what felt like a cracked rib as Eddie landed a punch to his side. Although wincing and winded, sheer anger brought the architect's fist around to Eddie's stomach.

Matt tried to drive him into the side of the building, hoping to shake him off and end this quick. The attempt was fruitless; Eddie was as immoveable as stone.

This was not looking good. The man was twice as big as Matt and seemed unhampered by concepts of clean fighting. Or sanity. Matt knew he was in deep.

Suddenly, a figure shoved into Eddie, sending him reeling across the sidewalk. A tall, broad-shouldered black man stood poised and ready, silently watching Eddie. The blow had enraged the worker. Eddie's wore a savage, distorted face as he turned to his attacker with an unarticulated scream.

Eddie lunged toward the stranger, swinging his fist like a hammer. But the new arrival gracefully dodged the blow and jabbed Eddie in the solar plexus in a single, practiced move.

Undaunted, Eddie grunted heavily and swung again.

Once more, the stranger's fist landed with maximum impact in Eddie's sensitive midsection. Eddie gave up fighting in any formal sense and merely lunged wildly, seeking only to return the pain.

The stranger, in a far more balanced stance, took advantage of Eddie's own momentum and sent him flying onto the sidewalk. The worker simply rolled and sprang back up, launching for a second attempt.

Seconds later, though, Eddie was face down with his hands behind him and the stranger's knee digging into his back. Each time the worker struggled, the man brought his arms up causing Eddie to howl in fresh pain.

Matt struggled to stand, gasping with each deep breath. He would be sore for a while, but mercifully nothing seemed broken. Matt watched as the other man calmly held the now restive Eddie down, but kept a wary eye on the group nearby.

"Come get your friend and cool him off!" Matt called to the men who were already rushing to Eddie's side.

The stranger stepped away from Eddie. Matt noted, however, the man never turned his back on the worker.

"Good timing. Thanks." Matt held out his hand after the group had disappeared inside. "Matt Wolf."

"You are just the man I am here to see." The newcomer stated, taking Matt's hand in a firm grip. "Jason Williams. I believe you are expecting me. I hunt ghosts."

15

As welcomes go, Jason reflected later as his team unloaded their rental van, *there's nothing like a brawl.*

Corvus Mound's main street was something out of time, a sleepy hamlet staring blankly at its own past like an old woman reminiscing. An old-fashioned drugstore (soda fountain and all) lay sandwiched between an honest-to-God shoe repair shop and a towering marquee heralding the Regent Theater. As his eyes followed the vertical sign downward, they came to rest upon a faded yellow square.

When was the last time you saw a sign for a fallout shelter, Jason?

His mind drifted briefly to the old school he attended as a child and the score of these signs that graced seemingly every surface. The universal symbol for radioactivity had always creeped him out. It looked too much like a cyclopsian jack-o-lantern grinning ominously through jagged teeth, a mutated harbinger of nuclear destruction

Beside him, his team was busy unloading cases filled with electronic equipment. Each lost in their own world, they worked efficiently and silently.

All of which was fine with Jason. He enjoyed the quiet. It gave him an opportunity to review their plans, see where any problems might crop up, and ask himself yet again why he had agreed to this idiotic video stunt.

Williams Investigations had not been as interesting or as colorful as their counterparts who regularly showed up on cable. They were not debunkers, but they strived to maintain scientific objectivity.

Over the years, Jason had found he had little tolerance for the charlatans who seemed to flock to the media.

Jason firmly believed that if there was something to the paranormal, then science would prove it, not some wild-eyed psychic on a rigged reality show.

Jason Williams flipped the notebook shut and tossed it to the top of the open box. His team worked quickly and efficiently around him in the main lobby; and not for the first time, he was thankful they were such a dedicated group. Their skills were the backbone of the operation and without them his investigations into supposed paranormal activities would evaporate.

This project was important, and he was betting the farm. He had put a lot of money into developing the prototypes for the systems his employee, Peter Evans, had designed.

Evans, a lanky young man with short, red hair and thick, dark-framed "Buddy Holly" glasses, could be an irascible prima donna, but his ideas were brilliant. Even in field tests, his prototype devices had yielded incredible results. But this hotel would be the big test of the entire system.

He recalled when he had first started on this peculiar path. Fueled by a couple of beers, Jason would play devil's advocate about so-called paranormal events with other cops. It was a bit of escapist fun after a long shift in a grim and all too real world. He kept suggesting rational explanations for every reported haunting, sighting, and strange thing that went bump in the night. One day, his buddies told him to put his money where his mouth was.

One thing led to another, and soon he was traveling a lot on weekends and off-duty days to investigate haunted houses. It was a just a hobby, a way to unwind from the pressures of his job.

Until his wife died.

Then hobby became obsession and his reputation as a merciless, cutthroat debunker began, due in large part to the Wilson-Maynard house.

The current owner of the one-time home of silent movie actor, Charles Wilson, told Jason that one particular room was always cold: cool in the heat of August and icy in the depth of winter. His terrier, Jake, would lay for hours on the floor outside that rooms, seemingly transfixed. However, the dog would never enter the room. The homeowner came to believe the room was haunted.

Jason arrived with his team to the now-boarded up Spanish Revival home in Hollywood at dusk. They inspected the structure, set up their equipment, and settled in for what was expected to be a quiet night.

In harsh tones of night-vision green, Jason's team watched for activity in and around the haunted room on several monitors in the garage. For hours, they gazed drowsily at what amounted to still images. However, just before midnight, the audio recording devices began picking up something that sounded like electrical static. The thermal sensors began to drop steadily until the air was strangely cold, and then the show really started. For a brief seven seconds the camera revealed a cluster of lights moving about the room.

Then it was over.

Everyone scrambled to evaluate his equipment, making certain everything was properly working. For the rest of the night, his ragtag team checked and re-checked instruments and sensors.

The event was not repeated, but it was a situation that left chills on anyone who thought about it. It whetted Jason's appetite for getting to the bottom of something he felt was understandable, if only it were identified.

After weeks of intensive on-site investigation, Jason pieced together evidence that pointed to a hoax, perpetrated quite artfully by the property owner. Additionally, Jason determined that a slight breeze blew just beneath the door to that room. In the summer the dog liked the cool breeze, and in the winter the icy air was a refreshing break from a furnace that kept the house stiflingly hot.

In a relentless, near-obsessive confrontation, Jason grilled the owner until he broke, spilling everything. He confessed to having orchestrated the "phenomenon" to drive up interest so that he could finally unload the place in a market where haunted homes were becoming more desirable as inns and B&Bs.

The press unfairly painted Jason as a "rogue cop" who had terrorized a confession from the hapless owner. He had sworn after that to keep a low profile in any future cases. They would come in, collect data, and then leave without a trace of their presence. Few interviews, no onsite tours with a psychic, and no séances. They were scientific, by-the-book, and dogged in their quest for rationality. Slowly, their mission gained a following and now their jobs were booked months in advance.

Unlike most amateur ghost hunters, Williams Investigations charged for their intensive, scientific appraisals of properties whose owners were less than thrilled at the thought of owning 'haunted' real estate. Not everyone, after all, is enamored with the prospect of owning "psychologically impacted" property. Many, he learned, were willing to pay for evidence debunking such claims. In time, Jason was earning enough to retire from the force.

Ruefully, Jason shook his head at his present situation. He realized all too well that money doesn't last. He was still committed to his standards of research, but the development of Peter's ideas had drained more of his savings than he cared to admit. If they were to develop and test Peter's work, they needed money. This is how

Williams Investigations came to Corvus Mound; they had a vision and Skyler Dunworth-Michaels had a check.

From the start, he had been zealous in his unwavering commitment to finding the truth. He knew if he just worked at it long enough and hard enough, that it would all come together. All this paranormal crap could be laid to rest and sensibility could replace the superstition that plagued so many. The certainty of his inevitable success was what made him get up to tackle a new day.

It was the only thing anymore. So if he had to trim his integrity some to accept the offer of a ratings whore like Skyler, it was justifiable—eventually.

"You are like a dog chasing a car, Jason darling..." sang a sweet Jamaican voice in his memory. Testament. The love of his life. Hidden in her smile were the magic of the rising sun and the mysteries of the moon.

"What are you going to do with it once you catch it? You have not thought this all out because you do not see, my love. What you want to discover has been there all along—just waiting for you to simply see it."

It was a frequent and familiar argument, pitting the dreamer against the pragmatist in a playful battle of words.

"And you," he said taking her warm body into his arms, "see too much. Take those charlatans you call for instance...."

"No! Jason, they are true psychics!" She had rebelled, as she always did, convinced that they were real while he had been equally convinced they were first rate con artists, milking suckers like his poor deluded Testament.

When she got sick a few short years ago, it was to healers she began to look instead of science. She was so convinced that she could be cured that, for a time, she did seem so vital and healthy.

Then he had come home one day and she had collapsed in the kitchen.

He listened to the doctor, concern etching deep grooves in her face, as she explained that the disease had gone unchecked too long. It was racing through her system, eating her alive and there was nothing they could do to stop it.

When he'd visited her a few days later in the hospital, Testament was still convinced that the potions and readings would help heal her. They had an argument and he had stalked out of her room angrily.

Hours later, he had crept back into the room to apologize, but it was empty. A note on the bed said she had heard of a healer back home in Jamaica who could help her. She had been able to contact him just that day.

I will see you soon and I will be healthy and we can play in the surf again like we did on our honeymoon.

He had taken the first flight to Kingston, but he was too late.

16

Peter Evans scurried through the empty rooms as quickly as he dared. He was almost through with his third round of readings for this floor, but it had to be done precisely. *Once those Neanderthals leave,* Peter thought disagreeably, *I can make a few more passes to get additional readings. Then feed it all into the program.*

"I'm finished up top." Jason called as he came down the stairs.

"Good. Right on schedule."

Stooping to pack one of the bags with leftover equipment, Jason asked: "Can you finish alone?"

"Sure, no problem."

"Carrie is about done with her equipment; I could send her up to help you?"

"No!" Peter said annoyed. "I'm fine." His mind was already running over the readings he was getting from the sensor clusters.

The automated sensors he and Jason had installed earlier would continue to take periodic readings throughout the night, establishing a baseline for later comparisons.

"See you downstairs then." Jason swept the area once more before heading down the stairs.

"Micromanaging Nazi," Peter muttered as the other man disappeared from view. Peace at last.

They could not understand or grasp the importance of his work. Without his software, his technology, and his methods, Williams Investigations would be mired in a morass of EMF meters and other pointless gadgets. Peter's work was a quantum leap in the field of paranormal investigation, eschewing the many archaic presumptions that held back the field for decades in favor of hard science.

The team wasn't all morons, he knew. Each member had some type of scientific or technical background—except for the big man himself. Jason lacked the sophistication to truly appreciate the demands of his own ideas.

For days, Peter had been busy charting every inch of these floors. He had created computer models of all the possible ways the air entered, how it flowed, and how it reacted to the internal environment of the hotel such as temperature, humidity, and ambient electrical fields.

The more they understood about the hotel's internal climate, the easier tracking anomalies became. In turn, this would provide the data to prove his theories correct.

It was all very delicate, very time consuming work. For example, this new program involved days of measurements, entering thousands of readings to develop a database, which the computer could draw upon for making comparisons and intuitive calculations.

Begrudgingly, Peter had to admit Williams was running the best operation in terms of testing this software and funding his research. Moreover, nobody else had the foresight to see the potential in Peter's vision.

After years of bouncing from group to group, Peter was sick of simple-minded, sloppy teams running through abandoned hospitals, wildly searching for "orbs." These clueless investigators could scarcely pull themselves away from their constant infighting to launch a truly successful investigation.

Suddenly a wave of anxiety, hot and acidic, churned like nausea, causing his head to go light and the room to spin like a wobbling top. It felt like a panic attack: unseen hands choked him as his lungs fought for air.

I'll never get done in time, he thought darkly. *There's no way. How did they expect me to work like this?*

He stumbled toward the hallway, clawing at his collar, seeking relief from the choking grip on his airway.

They didn't understand. No one ever did. There was so much to do....

He felt as if he were going to blackout; but as suddenly as it had come, it was gone.

Taking a deep breath, Peter felt the tension and rancor ebb. His head cleared, and once more he stood on steady legs.

"Shouldn't have passed up that burger at lunch," he rationalized out loud, if for no other reason to hear a voice—even his own. "Just low blood sugar."

Nearly two hours of hard work later, in some of the dustiest areas of the hotel, Peter set up the last sensor assembly in a remote hallway leading to the roof. He carefully placed the rest of his equipment in the black plastic storage tub at his feet and glanced at his watch. It was almost time to meet the others downstairs.

Don't know why I was even worried, he thought, remembering his earlier frustrations. *No problemo.* He shut the tub and turned toward the stairs, more than ready to find something to eat.

As an icy chill danced over his body, Peter instinctively stood motionless. Just through the open doorway to the stairwell, on the landing, a man stood. His shirt was wide open, revealing a jagged, blackened gash across his throat. Peter gaped as a small bubble of blood oozed out and dribbled down the man's bare chest, glistening in the feeble light reaching into the shadow-laced hall.

The eyes appeared to be little more than black holes, devoid of light. Yet, they weren't empty; something vile spilled from the man's sightless gaze. Peter felt nausea building within as a wave of violence and hatred crept toward him.

He backed up slowly until the wall behind him prevented any further retreat. Frozen with fear, Peter watched as the figure moved menacingly toward him. The motion set an old brass watch on the man's pants swinging on its chain like a pendulum.

"Oh, God! Oh, God!" Peter could only babble in growing fear as he slid along the wall, seeking escape.

Heart pounding, Peter ran down the hallway. Flinging himself and his gear down the stairs, he desperately sought refuge from the nightmare in which he now found himself.

It's not real, he kept telling himself. *It's not real!*

He dashed out into another hallway, skidding to a halt as he saw it was a blank wall. Breathing harshly, his eyes darted about like those of a panicked animal, searching wildly for his pursuer.

Peter shut his eyes. He tried to block out the vision, to forget that this was happening. It was useless; he could still see that ashen face and those horrible gouged out eyes. He swore he could hear that pocket watch ticking and could see the figure reaching out to him with a gurgling cry.

A sound from behind froze him where he stood. Careful to make no sound, he glanced backwards, expecting to see the apparition; but nothing stirred in the hall.

Peter slumped against the nearest wall. Sinking to the floor, he cradled his head in his hands as tears welled in his eyes. Beads of sweat gleamed on his forehead as a million explanations raced through his mind: overwork, stress, too many late nights....

Suddenly, another whisper of sound had him arching stiffly. Eyes wide, hardly daring to breathe, he searched every corner and shadow of the hallway. Taut and expectant, he listened as every creak and groan magnified his fear.

Another barely audible murmur launched Peter toward the stairs, toward the bright lights, and the sounds of the workers below.

17

A cacophony of shouts erupted from the men clamoring around the two combatants.

"Hit him, Randy!"

"Hey, you gonna take that?"

Thrusting himself past the spectators, Matt spotted two of the workers wrestling on the floor. Like Jackson Pollock canvases, each was covered in thick, overlapping layers of splattered paint.

Jedd Davis struggled with Jordan Myers, whom he normally looked on as the son he never had.

Matt had often seen the two together, laughing at some story or sharing the latest newspaper over lunch. Totally professional, Davis had always bragged that paint got on nothing but the walls when he worked. Now, to Matt's horror, a pool of red paint was soaking into the rug and spreading out like some horrible crime scene.

"I'll kill you! You damned mother—" Myers screamed up at the other man between blows. Davis was not only older and more experienced; he was also a good fifty pounds heavier than Myers.

Davis had pushed Myers dangerously close to the empty frame of a large picture window. Updrafts from the street below tousled the younger man's hair.

Matt picked up a nearby cleanup bucket and heaved it at the two men.

"Enough! That's enough, Davis!" Shoving the two apart, Matt raised his own fist in a preemptive move to halt the bigger man's approach. "Back off now, do you hear me? Now!"

The man seemed oblivious to anything but his own fevered desire to bash Myers' brain into the roses on the carpet.

Matt stepped between the workers, finding it was a struggle to hold the two back. One of Davis' fists briefly, but powerfully, connected with Matt's still tender ribs. Matt gasped in sudden pain as he felt his own anger begin to flare.

"Stop it!" he ground out harshly, shoving Davis back until the other man slammed into the wall where plaster tumbled down onto both of them.

"Just what the hell do you two think you're doing? Look at this mess! I don't know what your problem is—and I really don't care—but it stops now! I will not stand for bullshit like this."

The two men were separated but still glaring, chest heaving exhaustedly.

"Do you read me?" Matt demanded. A sour nod from Davis was his only reply. "Back off or both your asses are canned."

Matt angrily turned on the crowd at the doorway. "Somebody get these two clowns cooled off. I don't care if you have to put them in the freezer!"

Still glaring at one another, the two seemed on the brink of another explosion as they were pushed and dragged out of the room.

"Get back to work—all of you! If anything like this happens again, I will fire the entire crew on the spot. Now, go!"

The crew fled hastily from the room, leaving more grumbled protestations in their wake. Matt stared at the ravaged room in confusion.

Everybody had been different until this week. Maybe it's this heat. Maybe it's.... Matt recalled the altercation on the sidewalk earlier. Admit it, Matt, you don't have a clue what's going on.

"God, what a mess!" spoke a voice from behind. Jason Williams was looking around the room.

"Tell me about it."

"I heard all the noise and came up to see what was going on."

"I only wish I knew." Matt kicked a paint can out of his way. "I just wish I knew something. Anything."

"Does this kind of thing happen here often?" Jason motioned toward the disaster that had once been a nearly completed room

"What things? Oh, you mean two fights in as many days, two broken legs, a man in the hospital, missing tools…. No, I'd say that was pretty unusual for any worksite."

"Ah."

"Let's not forget the growing surliness and insubordination in the work crews."

"Is it always this hot here? This heat and humidity is enough to make a statue snarl. My team has been a bit on edge, as well."

"Heat stress pushing people to the limit? It's an idea. But, to tell you the truth, I've worked on far more grueling jobs and never witnessed this kind of behavior. Besides, these crews are all locals who should be able to handle the weather."

"Anybody in line to benefit from this project not getting finished? Competitors who could come in and conveniently pick up the pieces?"

"No, nothing like that." Matt stepped over to the window, surveying the damage.

"If what you say about such wholesale collapse being totally new in your experience," Jason mused. "There has to be a reason. Some motivating factor."

"You sound like a cop."

"I used to be. New Orleans"

"You mean before you became a ghost hunter?" Matt jibed. "I could see how the two might be a bit incompatible."

Jason laughed. "I take it you are not a 'believer'?"

Matt shook his head.

"Neither are we—not really." Jason admitted.

"I've got a feeling lots of people around here are leaning towards supernatural explanations. This afternoon I heard one of the crew talking about this place being haunted."

"Is that a common belief around here?" Jason asked. "What about you? Do you think this place is haunted or cursed?"

"I don't know. This project was my baby. I was planning on this job to really be the springboard to the kind of future I had wanted for a long time." Matt admitted ruefully. "Donaldson owns a lot of real estate; I could have written my own ticket with him."

"Well, you may have some headaches now, but the project isn't over yet." Jason offered as he exited the room.

As Matt watched him vanish among the shadows down the hall he heard a tiny voice in his head whisper, What's the use? You're a failure, just like your old man. Weak. Pathetic.

Matt stopped suddenly as the strident cry of a crow shattered the dark fugue that had gripped him. Matt realized in horror how dangerously close to the empty window frame he had stepped. The sill rose barely to his shins.

Perched on a decorative cornice near the ledge outside, a large black bird squawked in some unknown frustration.

God. One more step and I could have... Matt stepped gingerly back from the precipice.

In a sudden eruption of ebony feathers, the crow darted away, shrieking into the distance until the sounds of an ordinary work day once more filled Matt's ears.

18

"Among nearly three million artifacts in our collection, Karen, there is nothing remotely like this."

Karen was sitting in Dr. Henry Wellston's office at the University of Oklahoma. The overly large mahogany desk made the diminutive chief curator look almost childlike. Before him lay the sword Karen had unearthed the day before.

"I know," she replied emphatically. "That's why I wanted to bring this to you right away. This kind of contamination...."

The words were not necessary. They both understood the consequences.

"You're quite right about its resemblance to early Mesopotamian weaponry." The chief curator peered intently over the tops of his glasses. "It may, in fact, be an older Akkadian artifact. I'm sure that when Dr. Cicero returns he can shed some light on this."

"When will that be?" Karen chided herself for sounding so impatient with her boss.

"I'm afraid not until the end of the month. He's in the Middle East right now with that Egyptologist from Cairo, Dr. Jassim-Ali. I believe they are excavating the remains of a Nubian shrine at Giza with some fascinating—"

"Henry," Karen interrupted. "This is the second instance of possible contamination on this one site alone. If you remember, Miller found that rune stone in '57."

A large chuckle erupted from the small man. "What, the great Karen Houston doesn't believe Vikings visited pre-Columbian Oklahoma?"

Wellston would occasionally tease Karen, but she understood he was, in fact, one of those rare scholars who truly kept an open mind. Moreover, he was among her biggest supporters. His teasing was often a much-appreciated challenge to maintain her scientific objectivity.

"Despite my pet theories, Henry." Karen smiled. "I'm still a scientist. The Medok stone has never been conclusively authenticated. As for this Sumerian weapon...."

Wellston raised his hand to stop her. "I know, I know. It calls into question anything anyone has ever done to this site and mitigates the credibility of all future findings—including runestones."

Wearily, Karen slumped into the overstuffed chair facing Wellston's desk. "We need to keep a lid on this, Henry."

"I agree. But as a public institution, we can only do that for so long. Let's wait until Cicero gets back before we proceed. Take the sword back with you and keep it locked up." The man told her as he pushed it back across the smooth desktop. "Just don't let any of those over-zealous grad students catch sight of it. In fact, let's just shut the dig down for a couple of weeks and let them catch up on their site analysis."

"But we've only just begun to—" Even as she began, Karen felt the protest slip from her tongue. He was right. It was the only option for now. "Okay. I'll head back this afternoon."

19

After several days of heavy spring rains, the gray skies gave way to a stifling heat that lingered like an unwelcome guest. Humidity wrapped itself around the town, suffocating all but the most necessary of tasks.

Matt felt his freshly pressed shirt wilt as he stood on the sidewalk outside the Corvus Mound Archaeological Center.

So much for a good first impression, he thought dryly.

Driving out to the Center, Matt noticed life in Corvus Mound seemed to have slowed to a trickle. The traffic was non-existent and he had zipped out to the mounds in what must have been record time.

As the man on point, both the hotel's interior design and marketing firms had been breathing down his neck to find historic photos to complete the renovation and promote its historic status. He only hoped this kindly old woman would see fit to....

As a lithe, athletic brunette crossed the marbled floor toward him, his misconception regarding some little old lady happily vanished.

"Mr. Wolf? I'm Karen Houston." The young woman extended her hand. As the two shook, a quizzical look crossed her face. "Didn't I see you at the Get-Kwik a few days ago?"

"Yes." Matt responded with surprise. "I thought you looked familiar."

"Well, I hope you're enjoying your time here in Corvus Mound."

"Yes, I am. Thanks." Matt felt suddenly awkward. "I actually grew up around here. So, it's something of a homecoming."

"Please, come into the conference room." She said leading the way to a door just off the lobby.

Matt noted the heavy oak construction and the frosted glass were all original, but incongruous to the building's overall style. Salvaged, he figured.

"I've laid out some items I thought might be of interest to you." Karen indicated stacks of files and photographs spread out along the surface of an ornate Victorian conference table. "Have you been to the Center before?"

"No. This is my first visit." Matt looked around the room, "It's bigger than I expected."

"We just finished a simple display on the hotel's history, so finding material for you wasn't difficult."

"Sounds interesting." Matt stepped toward the table, picking up one of the photographs. It was the hotel at the height of its prominence. Clearly, an artist—someone with a keen eye for the dance of light and shadow—had had snapped the picture.

"A wife of one of the early manager's dabbled in photography," Karen explained. "I think some of these may be hers."

"They are fantastic." Matt picked up one of the copies, seeing something familiar. "Do you know her name?".

"Whitney," Karen told him, glancing at the file. "Margaret Whitney."

Matt picked up another, a detail of one of the wooden carvings Nancy had hated.

"Do you know why there are so many carvings and paintings of crows at the hotel?" Matt asked without looking up from the photograph.

"There are a lot of theories about that." Karen commented with a soft chuckle. "It could be that this area was once a nesting site for the birds. Or maybe because there was some kind of men's club working out of the hotel in its early days."

"Like the Masons?" Matt asked.

Karen nodded. "They must have been very secretive, but from what little I've learned, the crow was one of their symbols. Truth is, no one really knows."

"Well, I want to thank you, Karen." Matt picked up the copies she had made for him. "If there is anything I can do to help you in some way...."

"Not at all, Mr. Wolf. It was my pleasure."

"Matt."

"Sorry?" Karen spied him quizzically.

"Call me Matt."

"Well, it was my pleasure...Matt."

Matt proffered his hand, which she took warmly. He noticed—or perhaps hoped—that she seemed to linger a moment longer than necessary.

"If you want," he offered, "You can come by for our paranormal open house and see what all the fuss is about."

"Well, I don't know about ghosts. But I wouldn't mind seeing what you've done with the old place—as long as you don't think it will be too much trouble."

"Trouble? What trouble could there possibly be?"

20

April 27, 1926

So many little problems are cropping up. The staff is growing increasingly irritable and the cook had to separate two of the maids who were fighting. Gerald had asked me to check the rooms reserved for the Judge and his son. There had been so much to do today and poor Gerald was in a frenzied state.

Matt had been astounded when he heard Karen tell him the name of the photographer. The same woman who had written the journal he was reading. He'd planned to turn it over to the museum, but had become too engrossed in its pages.

It is as if the world were crumbling around us! I mentioned this to Gerald and he merely quoted one of the books he is always reading. He knows I do not understand them.... Today he merely said, 'sometimes to build you have to destroy.'

Despite his assurances that everything was under control, I sense such tension in him lately, almost a haunted look.

It seems that more and more, the burdens of life here are weighing him down. And me. Despite knowing powerful associates like Silas Montford, that horrid Judge Forbes, and the odious Senator Johnson....

Matt had scanned the pages of the diary into his laptop so he could read them more comfortably. They had proved more interesting than he could have imagined. He had been reading late into the night several days running now.

At first, they had been just quaint glimpses into the past of the fine old lady he was bringing back to life.

Then, when he had seen the world through her eyes in those photos, there was a sense of reality that was so strong he was stunned.

He had gone back to the hotel to read more of her thoughts. Quaint soon gave way to something far less innocent. Slowly, an unsettling image began to emerge.

21

The Corvus Mound main street was a wide thoroughfare that remained flat until it raced up the hill upon which the oldest buildings, including the Montford Arms, perched like pawns awaiting the first gambit.

At this hour of the day, the traffic had slowed to the occasional car and a few scattered pedestrians.

Ben Yellow Wolf leaned against the building, trying his best to look casual. He grinned, feeling a little like some cold war spy eyeing the Kremlin. He had been watching the hotel for the last half hour trying to get a feel for its comings and goings.

He had found several places where he might be able to slip in without being noticed. At least, he hoped that would be the case.

He had been afraid of being recognized and having to answer questions he had no idea how to answer. He had never been good at lying and didn't think he could do so now, which would mean coming across as a crazy old man should he get caught.

He wished he had been able to convince Matt to listen to him. Old men's stories, his father always said, get in the way of young men's dreams. He was afraid that was the case now.

That left him, a man whose bones creaked when he moved, to do the job.

22

Barely audible beneath the post-workday din at Marty's, was a faintly familiar classic rock tune. Matt tried to place it, but found the bar simply too noisy.

"Thanks," Matt said absently as the waitress brought his beer.

A couple of the regulars shouted a greeting as they herded companions to the booths along the walls. In the months he had been here, he had come to know many in the community, mostly at the bar. It was a refreshing break from the "liquid lunches" in Chicago filled with sycophantic poseurs kissing ass just to get an office with a window overlooking an office with a window. Here, there was no pretense: accountant, Timothy, sat joking with Paul, an oilfield worker with about an inch of mud encrusted on his work boots.

Matt enjoyed the casual atmosphere and had come to savor the times when he could just knock back a few beers with the current crew. Taking a deep swig from his beer, he decided he could get used to that.

A group of his men entered laughing. Despite the recent problems, Matt was encouraged that most still remained in good spirits. He hoped the surliness of a few didn't rub off on the rest.

"Matt, we're going to the back to shoot some pool," an electrician called out. "Wanna come?"

"Thanks," Matt replied, "But if you rob me at pool, I'll have nothing to pay you with."

"Hey, ya never know," the electrician countered. "This could be your night."

As the others emitted a rumble of agreement, Matt conceded.

After losing too many sets of pool and buying enough rounds of beer to justify leaving the men, Matt called it quits and began heading for the door.

Nearing the exit, though, he spotted Karen sitting at a corner booth toying with the drink in front of her. He swung by the bar for another beer before heading her direction.

"Mind if I joined you?" He asked.

"No, please. Sit." Karen smiled, as she moved her carryall from the other bench.

"Would you like another drink?" He asked, looking toward the bar.

"No, I'm fine. Thanks."

"So...." Matt was unsure how to proceed. He took a nervous swig from the bottle. "I think I may be just drunk enough to...." He paused to collect his thoughts.

"Matt, I really don't think you should," she teased. "That is, we hardly know each other."

"NO!" He cried a little louder than intended. "No," he said more softly. "I don't mean *that*. I mean," Matt tried hard to focus. "There are things I need to tell you about the hotel."

"Oh, the *hotel*."

"What I mean is there are things I need to tell you."

"About the hotel?" She laughed and then relented. "Okay, tell me about the hotel."

"Right. Listen to me, the lady in the museum is in the diary. Well, not her but her mom, but she told me and that's how I know. There's stuff in there that—"

"Wait, hold on!" Karen urged stopping the edgy rush of words. "Slow down a little bit. One thing at a time."

Composing his thoughts, Matt began again. "Remember when you found those photos we needed? You said some were taken by Margaret Whitney."

"Yes, she was the wife of an early manager."

"Right," he stated before sinking the last drop of beer. "Well, I found something hidden in the hotel."

Karen's face grew more serious. "What did you find?"

"Her diary."

"Really?" Karen sat up, focusing intently on Matt. "What's in it?"

"She writes about some strange things that happened."

"You mean…." She asked, begging for confirmation. "You gotta be kidding!" Karen smiled broadly at him. However, one look and she knew he was serious. "Okay, for this I need another drink."

Matt motioned for another round as he tried to marshal his thoughts.

"According to her diary, she had witnessed the same types of accidents and quarrels that are now plaguing my crew."

"Are you saying the place is cursed?" Seeing the earnest expression on his face, Karen tried her best to suppress a smile. "Matt, a hotel can be a busy place. I'm sure that a lot of fights have cropped up over the years."

"I don't know what I'm saying." Matt felt a little embarrassed now that the words hung in the smoky air between them, but he needed a sounding board.

The glossy image of the Channel 6 reporter, Skyler Dunworth-Michaels, appeared on the bar's television screen, breaking the uncomfortable silence that had settled over their conversation.

All week, the station had been airing a commercial for Skyler's upcoming special that promised to salaciously reveal the hotel's sordid past and explore its 'horrific haunting'. The previous night's promo featured a muddle of hype and innuendo concerning a "disaster-plagued" remodeling effort that just skirted being libelous.

"History is your thing," he told Karen finally. "I have nothing concrete to verify those stories."

"And you probably won't find anything." Karen replied. "Stories like that probably cropped up while the hotel sat abandoned."

Matt focused, trying to shake off the effect of the many beers he had been downing all night.

"She started that journal in the twenties," Matt countered.

"I just don't think you can take it that seriously." Karen tried to encourage him and keep her own mounting frustration with this unusual conversation at bay. She wasn't doing a good job.

"Maybe I am making too much out of this, but when my grandfather...." Matt caught himself. From somewhere deep within his inebriated consciousness, a voice of reason rose weakly. *For God's sake, don't tell her about that!*

"Matt?" Karen looked at him quizzically. "You okay?"

Matt shook his head, hoping to rattle free some clearer thoughts.

"Yeah. I just think there are a lot of similarities, that's all." Sensing her growing discomfort, Matt shifted gears. "I guess I'm grasping at straws. It's just been so unusual around there lately, and when I read those horrible stories in that diary...."

"Fights among the workers?"

"No," Matt replied slowly, his voice dropping lower. "It gets worse."

"Oh?" Karen's waning interest was once more piqued.

"One of the entries concerned room 422 where the son of some big shot beat up a prostitute, I think. Anyway, the girl's body was found by the trash bins the next day, wrapped in a hotel rug. The police labeled it a suicide."

Karen glanced up from her beer, "God, how awful."

"Margaret wrote that the staff started having knockdown fights, too. There was talk of ghosts and bad luck. One of the maids even threatened a cook with a knife! The thing is, Karen, it's too much like the stuff I'm dealing with to ignore."

"You know, Matt, there's been talk in town over the years," Karen said. "Nothing in print, really. Just small town legends about some of the shady characters that used to call the hotel home."

"I never heard about those."

"Small town scandals are often swept under the rug."

"Reading those entries." Matt shook his head. "I don't know…. It seemed like more than just dirty laundry. I felt like there was something foul there, something tainted. All that anger, fear, and fighting."

Karen nodded. "You think it's happening all over again?"

Matt shrugged as he glanced at Skyler Dunworth-Michael's face still looming on the TV over the bar.

"I hope I haven't scared you off." Matt attempted a weak laugh. "You're still coming, right?"

"To the hotel's paranormal grand opening?" she asked lightheartedly. "I wouldn't miss it for the world—as long as there's food."

"There will definitely be warming trays. I can't guarantee what you find inside will qualify as food. But if you are feeling adventurous...."

"I'm always up for an adventure," she chuckled. "Besides, what's the worst that could happen? Indigestion? Please, I've eaten at the *Get-Kwik* I can handle anything I find in your hotel."

23

Skyler Dunworth-Michaels swept into the hotel with a leather weekender hanging from one shoulder. Whipping the sunglasses from her face, she looked around the foyer in approval as her crew spilled in behind her, hefting cameras, lighting, and sound equipment.

The plump woman who shuffled in next, tugging a reluctant pilot case, was a familiar face to anyone who had waited in line at the grocery store. Carol "Cookie" Daniels' aging features—with her signature pink suits, blue eyeshadow, and voluminous cloud of cotton candy hair—had been on magazine covers ranging from *People* to *The National Enquirer*.

An advisor over the years to both politicians and pop stars, Daniels had been featured on several television shows. Her melodramatic and often tearful "readings" of a place played well with the angels-among-us crowd or those who saw a demonic visage in their water-stained ceiling.

Now, however, she looked like any travel weary, slightly disoriented tourist stumbling in from the midday heat.

In contrast, the woman in stark leather stalking in after her seemed totally out of place. Her metal-plated biker boots clanked across the floor as she followed the others. A wicked spiked dog collar added a dangerous note. With her headphones, and long ebony hair, Shade was, as usual, a post-apocalyptic Morticia Addams.

Skyler's ever-growing mountain of matched Louis Vuitton luggage contrasted sharply to the single beat-up duffel Shade wore slung across one shoulder. Its ancient canvas seemed to be held together by a collection of pins, patches and buttons with slogans ranging from "My Dragon Ate Your Honor Student" to "I don't do tans."

"All here?" Skyler asked finally with a forced lilt, taking a place beside the registration counter. Following close to her, juggling equipment, were her two cameramen: Scott Linwood and Alex Davies.

Shade sized up the two men who wore the obvious scars of working under the yoke of someone like Skyler Dunworth-Michaels.

Alex was a short, chubby young man with features so nondescript that, if he stood still long enough, he could disappear into the landscape unnoticed, like a chameleon. Whereas, Scott's bald, muscular form was barely contained within his snug jeans and thin Channel 6 t-shirt, which stretched tautly across his broad frame.

Shade was instantly distracted, appreciating the latter with a long and thirsty gaze. She could see why Skyler kept the six-foot, tattooed Mr. Clean around: the prom queen likes them rough.

Once certain she had command of everyone's attention, Skyler opened her attaché and extracted the weekend's agenda.

"How soon can we get to our rooms?" Cookie complained, accepting her copy of the schedule. "I really need to freshen up. I'm not used to this humidity."

Taking notice that she may have grumbled with more fervor than intended, Cookie shifted gears. Assuming her usual perky demeanor, she added, "It's just that when dealing with the spirits, one must be in a relaxed, comfortable state."

"I find eighty proof spirits always relax me," Shade offered.

Scott barked a laugh that he quickly changed into a cough, as Skyler shot him a frigid look. Although Scott recognized Skyler's reprimand, he couldn't help sending Shade a conspiratorial wink. Like a pair of mischievous school children, they grinned at each other.

"Returning to the agenda...." Skyler stopped as she noticed Jason and his crew enter the lobby. "Ah, good. Mr. Williams is here."

Jason, ever serious, took up a stance along one wall and crossed his arms for business. Taking a cue from their leader's attitude, the rest of his crew casually straddled chairs or slumped onto the sofa.

"Decided I didn't want to miss introductions, after all," Jason spoke dryly. "Please, continue."

"This is my team from Channel 6 News: Alex Davies and Scott Lynwood." The men nodded in turn.

"And..." Skyler motioned to the woman in the rumpled pink suit, "Cookie Daniels, who needs no introduction, has agreed to join us this weekend." The woman in question regally bowed her head in response. The attempt at composure only emphasized her overall wan condition. "If for some strange reason you aren't aware, Cookie has worked with movie stars, Fortune 500 CEO's, and even several presidents."

Cookie beamed as bright as her brilliant pink suit. Her smile quickly faltered as she took note of the many blank faces that now unblinkingly appraised her.

"Over here," Skyler continued. "We have Roberta—"

"It's *Shade*," the goth spoke emphatically.

"*Shade* Hoffmeyer," Skyler seethed obsequiously through a forced smile before continuing, "is also part of the psychic investigation this weekend. The station thought she would make an *interesting* addition to this weekend."

Shade rolled her eyes at the woman's condescending tone.

Jason shoved himself away from the wall.

"I am Jason Williams," the investigator spoke, quickly preempting any introduction from the reporter. "I run Williams Investigations and this is my team: Peter, Richard and Carrie." He indicated the two men; one slumped morosely into on the sofa and the other languidly straddled a straight-backed chair. Seated more properly nearby, was a mousy young woman who kept pushing up her dark rimmed glasses.

"Jason will explain more about them a little later." Skyler reasserted. "For now, let's get down to business. As I indicated in my emails Mr. Donaldson has given us until Sunday night to conduct our little project."

Shade sensed her voice took on a peculiarly satisfied tone when she spoke Donaldson's name.

"Each of you has been hired for a special project: to investigate claims of paranormal activity in this hotel. Hopefully, my guys will catch something on camera." She indicated the two men at her periphery.

"Mr. Wolf has set up rooms for us and arranged for food to be brought in. It's mostly serve yourself, I am afraid—except for tonight. We are having a buffet delivered to get us started!"

Skyler scanned her checklist once more. "You will have rooms on the third and fourth floors. Here are the ground rules." She handed them each a sheet of paper with a list of regulations. "And remember: no one will be allowed to leave after midnight."

"Ooh...." Shade drawled as she rubbed her hands together in mock excitement. "A lock-in!"

"To do this right," Jason announced, ignoring the comment, "the area must be secured."

"Absolutely," the reporter agreed. "Read the small print in the contracts you signed—you leave...you lose."

"So," Scott added, "we gotta check that all the gear is in before midnight. Me and Alex can help if there's anything you still need."

"Yes, before midnight," Skylar emphasized. "After that, Mr. Wolf tells me the electronic locks are activated. Yes, before you ask, he will be here to unlock them in case of any emergencies."

"My crew," Jason interjected, "has set up have their equipment in the basement, the lobby, and on each of the floors."

Turning towards the guest psychics, Skyler continued. "Shade and Cookie, you can roam wherever you like as long as a cameraman is with you."

"I may be jumping the gun here," Cookie interjected breathlessly. "But, I do have some experience in these things. I think we should concentrate on the known hot spots."

"Great idea, Cookie!" Skyler exclaimed, bathing the older woman in her award-winning smile. "That will be a great help. Perhaps you two can work together? A dueling psychics kind of thing?"

Cookie and Shade shot each other equally appalled looks.

"We'll split up," Cookie answered without hesitation.

"Great! As you two go about your routine for the next couple of days, my guys will be following with the cameras." Skyler turned to Williams next, "Jason, would you care to explain how your team will work?"

"What we are trying to do here." Jason began, "is give scientific reasons for the phenomena reported here over the years."

Making his way to the front of the group, he added, "To that end, we will be setting up thermal sensors, motion detectors, and an assortment of other electronic equipment. These are all designed to map the nuances of this structure, no matter how minute they may be. It's our belief that most things can be explained in very prosaic terms once enough data is present."

"My assistants here," he continued, nodding toward the group clustered at the back, "are the real experts in these areas."

"Peter Evans' field is microclimatology." Jason explained. "He'll be charting the air flow, temperature, and humidity in the building."

Continuing the lineup, Jason introduced a young Asian man as Richard Simms, the electronics expert who would handle their small but complex network of computers and specially designed software.

Watching him smack his gum and straddle his chair backwards, Shade thought Simms hardly came across as a cold, scientific professional.

Cool.

Then, coming to his final member, Jason introduced a rather studious looking grad student named Carrie Pierce. She held her head shyly, hair cascading like a veil across her face. Her eyes were hidden behind thick, greasy lenses. Jason explained that she was the team's video expert who came outfitted "with enough equipment to make NASA jealous."

"She will document using thermal, night-vision, and spectrographic imaging."

"Why would you need a microclima...cli...?" Cookie asked, interrupting Jason's introductions.

"In order to know what is normal and abnormal about things that happen, such as the 'cold spots' so often reported in such situations, we have to get a picture of the climate in this building. It's really just small scale meteorology."

"Oh, okay. I think I understand," Cookie said. She didn't understand at all. "Can we go to our rooms now?"

"Yes, well I suppose the rest can wait until dinner," Skyler said. "Probably by the time you have freshened up and we've done some preliminary work, the food will be ready. Let's all meet down here at seven for dinner."

"Thank God!" Alex's voice was scarcely more than a whisper. "I only had gas station gourmet for breakfast."

"Oh yes," Skyler added as she grabbed an envelope from the counter. "One last thing...."

She opened the packet and spilled a handful of surprisingly old fashioned brass keys affixed to a tag bearing their room numbers.

"Here are your room keys." She handed one to each of the new arrivals. "You can drop off your bags and freshen up, but I need you guys back here in an hour."

Shade took the proffered key, rolled it in her palm, and then read the number on the tag: 422.

Once everyone had a key, they hefted their bags and headed up the main stairs in search of their rooms.

"Dammit, Scott, I want those set up along the back wall!" Skyler shrieked, her voice trailing off as the others mounted the grand staircase, swallowed by the gloom above.

24

After paying the caterers, Matt headed to the kitchen with an armful of hot trays that unfairly reminded him he had once again skipped lunch. His stomach growled angrily. Checking his watch, he saw there was not time for a bite if he wanted to secure the hotel after the last crew left.

His cell phone buzzed. Looking down, he was surprised to see Rick Donaldson's number.

"Mr. Donaldson. What can I do for you?"

"Please, Matt, how many times do I have to tell you to call me Rick?" Donaldson's voice held the reproachful timbre of a sit-com dad. "I just wondered if you'd thought anymore about my offer."

"I have, but the project has taken a lot of my time lately. I'm sorry I didn't get back to you sooner."

"I understand. The offer still stands. Whenever you are ready to discuss it, just give me a buzz."

"Thank you, sir—Rick."

"I could really use a man with your potential and talents in my camp."

"Rick... I must admit I'm intrigued. I have always wanted a position with the creative license and resources you mentioned. It's just...."

"You are a man of integrity and don't feel comfortable leaving Rand in the middle of a job? Is that it?"

"You're a mind reader."

"No, just lots of experience tempting the best." Donaldson made a small sound that Matt took to be a laugh. "I'll tell you a little secret, Matt. I will soon make Mrs. Rand an offer that I think she will have a lot of trouble turning down. When that happens, I'll be looking for some new blood."

Again, Donaldson chuckled softly. It was a laugh that left Matt feeling inexplicably troubled.

25

Shade followed Jason up the main stairs. He moved effortlessly as he carried two heavy bags. She found herself enjoying the view of his muscles as they undulated beneath his snug shirt.

As they traveled along the second floor corridor, they both scanned room numbers, until finally Jason set his bags down in front of number 419. Shade noted his proximity and decided to break the ice.

"Almost roomies," she grinned as she fished the key from her pocket.

"Guess so," he responded without any enthusiasm.

Shade, a little off-put, was about to say something when she put the key into the lock and let out a sudden gasp.

A sudden jolt of psychic energy shot through her as she gripped the old door knob.

Damn! she thought to herself. Not here...not now. Erratic images flickered wildly through her mind with strobe light intensity. Incomprehensible colors and shapes danced through her head.

This room....

Bodies twisted in savage ecstasy, writhing on a bed. Lust that turned into something else, something more virulent in its need and urgency.

A dark hunger.

A woman sobbed.

Pain.

A man smeared his naked torso with two bloody hands. Shadows emerged from walls to spin like dervishes, consuming the light. The man looked directly at her—through her—before bursting into flame and scattering in all directions like shards of glass.

The scene shifted abruptly, like the sudden downward assault of a rollercoaster. Shade's stomach churned. Shade now saw Jason on a long white ribbon of sand. A woman laughed as she danced into jewel-toned water, her mahogany legs kissed by the foaming surf.

Laugh, the woman commanded with teasingly.

Testament! He called after her, a look of fear on his face.

Ripping her hand and mind free from the door, Shade turned with exhaustion.

"Too many images...." she said aloud in an unexpected need to speak. "Something dark here."

Seldom did she feel such a strong sensation. Everything seemed more intense and accelerated. Remembering the almost intrusive images of the man across the hall, she paused deciding not to reveal the rest. "This room was part of it all. I think...a woman was violently raped here by a young man."

"You know," Jason spat, flinging a suitcase through his open door. "People like you make me sick!"

Shade staggered, shocked at this unexpected assault.

Teach me to open my big mouth, she thought ruefully.

She should have known it was never safe to let her guard down. Hadn't she learned long ago that the real Shade—the woman with the freaky abilities—had to stay hidden?

"Look at you!" Jason snarled as his eyes scanned her appearance scornfully. "Halloween was over months ago."

Shade stepped backward, defensively.

"No matter where we've gone, there's always someone like you, slobbering to be in front of the camera or quoted by some idiot like Skyler. Well, there aren't any cameras here, so you can drop the act. Nobody's impressed!"

Snapping out of her shock, Shade pasted the attitude back on and tossed her dark hair, eyeing the man in well-practiced derision. She had spent years wearing this mask to protect her from people like this. Deep down, though, Shade also felt an unexpected pain at the injustice of it all. Oh, well....

"Aww," she drawled patronizingly. "Do you need a nap? I hear, as you get older...."

"Don't even try to pull your psychic shit on me this weekend."

"Well, you're in luck; I can't read your mind if you don't have a brain," Shade spat out snidely.

"We know every trick. We will break you if you try anything, anything at all."

"Ugh!" she groaned. "I'm bored with you already!" Shade punctuated her statement with a dramatic yawn. "But I can see why *Testament* wanted you to laugh."

"Where did you get that name?" Jason growled, slamming a fist on the doorjamb and blocking her with his body. He was every inch the cop, as he demanded a response. "Answer me. Where!?"

Shade felt his body heat, sensed his power and strength, as he strained for an answer.

"Remember?" she spat out, slipping under his arm. "I'm psychic!"

She slammed the door.

Once inside her room, Shade let out a sigh, as she slumped wearily against the door. She suddenly felt very lonely and very angry.

She should have known better than opening up like that. *Don't get too close*, she told herself. It was a principle that served to protect her both emotionally and psychically.

Truth was, she had opened up before and it was far from a disaster. It's that uncertainty that always makes it so difficult, she mused bitterly.

Priscilla Jade Thomas, the wise woman who had taken an angry girl in from the streets, mentoring her in the ways of....

No. She had been a mother. There was no other way to phrase it.

And, of course, Kevin—her best friend and fellow ogler of men.

These were the two closest people in her life and yet, at times, she felt she could not open up fully to them either. There was just so much more they did not know. There was still so much she did not understand herself. At times, she felt like a victim to her own power, which made it all the more difficult when people like Jason Williams....

Shade shook off her momentary self-pity and threw her duffle on the bed. Grabbing hold of a small charm resembling a Raggedy Ann voodoo doll, she unzipped the bag, and unceremoniously dumped its contents: a few shirts, another pair of jeans, some underwear—black, of course—and other essentials.

Stripping off her travel-weary shirt, she began rummaging for a replacement. She settled on a vintage tee emblazoned with the logo of an obscure punk band, checked to see her dog collar was in place, and set out to really connect with the hotel.

26

Matt watched silently from a chair by the window in the hotel office as Nancy flipped through the bills he had given her. The celebrated Queen of Minutiae loved to micromanage every conceivable detail. This would take a while.

The office overlooked the gardens in the rear of the hotel where they had just finished repairs to the old stone paths that wound through the newly-planted landscape. The lotus-shaped fountains once more shot streams of water in the air and the ponds would soon be filled with fat, little koi. It would have been a good place to watch the guests without being seen. Matt wondered how many lazy afternoons had been wasted doing just that.

He sat back into the large leather wingback and allowed his mind to drift. His eyes lighted upon the strange, old sword affixed to the mantel above the fireplace. He admired its gilded hilt and the strange blade that widened toward the center.

That would look pretty sweet over my fireplace at home.

In fact, Matt had admired many of the old furnishings left behind in the office, which is why he had commandeered the space for himself. Part of the appeal was that the room contained a secret panel that opened to reveal a hidden staircase. The passage descended to the basement kitchen and rose to a suite on the fourth floor. He supposed the suite had been the manager's living quarters.

"Good work, Matt."

Nancy's voice shattered his restful musings and he sat up with a start.

"These are all under budget," she continued. "Of course, I wouldn't expect anything less from you."

"Thank you." Matt was surprised. He couldn't remember Nancy ever offering a compliment before.

"Damn." She sighed with a sudden sense of resignation, as she shifted uncomfortably in her chair. "I might as well get this over with."

Matt shot her a nervous glance, fearing the words to come.

"There's something I've been meaning to do for some time."

Uh oh.

"I've never been very good with people," she continued. "Too much brass, I've been told. For twenty years I've been running this company since my husband died. Wasn't easy, but I couldn't afford to fail with the debt he left me. Anyway, Matt I want you to know that things will be changing soon." She took a deep breath and then stated baldly, "I'm retiring this year. I'm handing the business over to someone who has the imagination, the know-how, and the energy to make it something very special. I'm handing it over to you, Matt."

"You're what?" Matt couldn't believe he had heard correctly.

"My lawyers have drawn up the paperwork. Everything will be in your control as soon as you go back to Chicago and sign on the dotted lines."

"I—I don't understand. How can you…"

"The accountants have gone over the books and tell me we are in good shape. Largely due to you, but I can still take some credit there too."

"Nancy! You have to be pulling my leg. There's no reason for you to retire this soon."

"Well, the doctors tell me different. The old ticker has seen a bit too much mileage for the stress I've put it under. That's what they tell me anyway. So I'm retiring to enjoy the life I worked like hell to have for the time I have left. Life's a bitch sometimes and that's the truth."

For the first time in his association with the woman, she looked vulnerable and old. She seemed to diminish for a moment, sagging into soft lines and then it was gone. The mouth was once more a firm slash across her face and her back straight.

"Anyway, that's my sad story. I'm leaving this to you. If I'd been stupid enough to have children…. Well, one of them might have turned out like you. I know Donaldson has been sniffing around trying to lure you away, but you are too good for his kind of business. You have too much soul. What you do with all of this will be your decision. But, please, don't sell it to Skippy until I'm cold in the ground. If you do, by God, I swear I will come back and haunt you!"

"I don't know what to say…." The size of Matt's eyes equaled that of his gaping mouth. He couldn't even begin to process what had just happened.

"Well, just shut your mouth and go see if Sattler has that kitchen in order."

It seemed to Matt, just for an instance, Nancy Rand suppressed a smile.

"Shoo! Go! Get to work!"

27

Nancy charged up the stairs to check with Jones who was working at the far end of the second floor.

As she climbed, she could hear the noisy movements of Donaldson's guests in the lobby. She wanted to be as far away from them as possible. *Leave that to Matt*, she thought, *delegation has its benefits*. If she was lucky, she would be out of the hotel before they were set loose.

In the bath of 203, a young plumber lurked over the shoulder of a bony, gray-haired man. Hawk-like, he watched as the aged mentor attempted to fasten a shiny length of copper into place. A faded t-shirt that read *Plumbers Have The Biggest Tools* hung from his gaunt frame.

In your dreams, Nancy thought.

Seeing her at the door, Jones straightened, hitched up his worn jeans, and called out a greeting.

"I hope you've got good news." She looked around. "Because it's too late for coffee and too early for booze."

"Well, considerin' the age of the building, all the major pipes are lookin' real good. Some of the new additions were cheap shit—excuse my French—but the old part was built solid."

"That's what I like to hear."

"All those special replacements we talked about should be done as soon as we get back from the holiday."

"Good. If you see Matt, tell him I'm going up top to check out that deck project. If I have time, I'll probably poke around the upper floors as well."

"Will do, boss."

Nancy turned on heel, exited the room in her typical military fashion, and charged up the stairs to the dark recesses of the topmost floors.

28

"There's a small glitch in sensor 12-R7-E1," Richard commented absently.

Once Jason Williams's team had finished setting up the last of the equipment and several calibration tests were run, they began the time consuming task of charting every square foot of the Montford Arms.

As soon as the word was given, the system began compiling data on temperature, humidity, airflow, air pressure....

All this was to establish the average environmental conditions at the hotel. Once the data had been fed into the computer, it would then be able to run rapid-fire calculations to alert them of potential anomalous activity. This would also activate Carrie's array of visual sensors, which worked on a multitude of wavelengths, much like a satellite.

"Yeah, yeah," Peter responded with a dismissive wave. "I'll get on it. It's not like you were out there helping me set and calibrate all seven-hundred fifty of these!"

"Chill, dude. I just said it was a little wonky."

With a pursed look, the microclimatologist checked the laptop feed. "Can you give me a diagnostic while it's still compiling?"

"Yeah, hold on." Richard typed a series of commands and another window popped up on the screen. Instead of a sleek, well-designed database, this was a crude litany of code and it piqued Peter's interest.

"What is it?" Carrie asked as she entered their corner of the lobby.

"There's a glitch in a sensor on the fourth floor, but Peter may be onto something. I think."

"You're damn right!" Peter cried out excitedly. Snatching the small two-way radio from the table, he signaled for Jason.

"Yeah, Pete. What's up?" Jason's voiced echoed with static throughout the cavernous lobby.

"I know it's early, but I think I may have something. It seemed like a glitch but I've run diagnostics on the unit and there's no problem."

"What is it?"

"Seems like," Peter quickly checked the system again. "Seems like some sort of subsonic frequency. It's very regular."

"Keep tracking it and get me a seismic cross-check. I want to know if this is the workers or something outside, near the hotel."

"I'm on it."

The team quickly moved about their computers, attempting to isolate and distinguish the anomaly.

"Sir," Carrie spoke into her own two-way. "I've processed audio on it; it's below human hearing, but I've beefed it up some."

"Play it."

Carrie broadcast the audio over the speakers while pressing down the "talk" button on her radio. A deep, droning hum could be heard filling the entire lobby. She quickly ran the file through a series of filters to clean it up.

"Carrie," Jason called out. "It's pretty rhythmic. Could it be construction?"

"I'll go out and check around." Carrie grabbed a portable sensor and headed toward the main doors.

"I want you guys to keep tracking this. Let me know if you find anything else. I'll go check to see if there are any workers left and let Skyler know."

"On it, Jason." Peter said and then he set down the radio and focused intently on the anomaly.

"What do you think it is?" Richard asked.

"Probably just something in this old hotel vibrating, but that alone is exciting."

"Why?"

"Well," Peter continued, losing all trace of rancor. "Studies have shown certain frequencies can affect the human eye, causing hallucinations. Also, subsonic vibrations can have an effect on the nervous system. Some people can feel 'afraid' with the proper sonic stimulus. If we can prove that such a thing is happening here, it would help explain some of these claims."

"Nice theory," Richard said, shedding some of his lethargy. "So, I take it you don't believe this place is haunted either?"

"Hell no!" Peter replied once more with a sharp tone. "Don't be a tool."

What is Peter's problem lately? Richard fumed. *Ever since we pulled into town, he's been an asshole. He can't still be pissed about that chick at Paul's party? This is going to be a long weekend.*

29

Nancy Rand's inspection of the upper floors progressed more rapidly than she had anticipated. After visiting the fourteenth floor to determine whether a rooftop terrace was a wise idea, Nancy glanced at her watch and realized she had time enough to give the lower levels another glance.

Her heart thudded in her chest as she trudged down the stairs. Briefly, she wondered if she had forgotten to take her pills again.

When is that damn elevator going to get fixed, she wondered. *I'm too old for this.*

As she arrived at the tenth floor, she spotted a man standing still in the shadows halfway down the hall.

Startled, she paused. Something in the way he just stood there made Nancy keenly aware of her own isolation. She could no longer hear the clamor of workers or the noise of traffic on the street below. There was only the sound of her pounding heart to fill the silence.

Moving suddenly, the figure turned to look at her. The eyes were vacant, shadowy holes. As she stared, transfixed, a vice tightened viciously around her chest.

Oh, God....

Dragging in huge, desperate gulps of air, her hand clawed instinctively for the phone in her pocket.

Even as she clutched it to her head, the thing in the hall began to shift. The figure was changing, becoming wispy and insubstantial enough to reveal a painting on the wall beyond. She could feel him—it—picking through her head, pilfering her thoughts. A powerful headache blossomed suddenly as a dull thrum filled her senses.

Frantically, Nancy glanced at the keypad to dial for help; but when she lifted her eyes, the figure was gone. The space in front of the painting was now totally empty.

Turning, she suddenly screamed as she found him standing only a few feet away. His appearance was now more substantial and threatening. She could clearly see his blood-splattered shirt.

Without warning, his cadaverous hand thrust out, pushing with it an icy burst of air.

Staggering backward into the wall, Nancy felt her heart thudding suddenly in great spasms of fear. She struggled to breathe.

"No! Go away!" she screamed in terror.

As she launched herself past him, toward the stairwell, Nancy stumbled out of her left shoe. She kicked both off impatiently as she darted away, ignoring the sudden ache in her ankle.

"Help!" she screamed hoarsely when she reached the top stair. She was sure that right behind her, dogging each frantic step, was the strange and horrible vision. She couldn't bring herself to look.

With each step downward, her fear-weakened legs threatened to give out. Once again, she fumbled with the phone until she had Matt's number. She jabbed the send button.

"Get me out of here!" she cried, tears streaking her face. The clenching pain was making her light headed. She was struggling to maintain both her balance and momentum when her bare foot caught in a curled seam of carpet.

Tottering for a fierce moment, she clawed desperately at the air. Finding no hold, Nancy Rand tumbled headfirst down the stairwell.

30

Trotting up the last few steps, Shade paused for Scott to catch up on the seventh floor landing. Ahead of her stretched a long hallway darkened by panels of rich wood and old transom-topped doors. The smell of new carpet and fresh paint thickly permeated the air.

Scott clattered up the last steps, heaving in an exaggerated manner, as he propped the camera on his knee and glared at her.

"A bit out of shape, are we?" Shade asked, turning to head down the hallway at a brisk pace.

"It's not a race," he panted. "We've got all weekend!"

Shade simply egged the man on with a wicked grin.

"I just wish they'd get the elevators fixed." He groaned between exhausted huffs. "This is inhuman!"

"Inhuman?" Shade laughed. "It's only the seventh floor!" Then, after a pause, she added, "I guess we could have taken the dumbwaiter."

"I wouldn't complain," Scott sputtered.

"The exercise was good for you." She grinned over her shoulder.

Shade was lightly touching door knobs as she swept through the hall. *Very lightly*, she thought, remembering her earlier experience. No double-feature horror scenes greeted her this time. There were only images of half-forgotten moments dancing across her consciousness: happy couples, tired business men, forbidden trysts, complaining maids, the cries of weary infants....

"Can I get some up shots?" Scott called, halting her in mid-stride.

"Up what, exactly, are you wanting to shoot?" Shade darted Scott a challenging look before her pursed lips melted into a flirtatious grin.

"I'm a gentleman, Ms. Hoffmeyer." Scott feigned insult as much as possible, but he could tell by the look on her face that she didn't buy it.

"Just remember," Shade spoke in a soft, serious tone. "I don't want my face on camera."

Shade liked Scott, but she reminded herself that he worked for Skyler. It took no clairvoyance to know that woman wasn't to be trusted.

Scott motioned her further down the hall as he attempted to find better lighting.

"What's this?" he asked, indicating an ornately framed oil painting. "Kinda creepy for a hotel, don't you think?"

The tableau featured a parched landscape scarred by dark swaths of paint.

"I'll see if they've got prints in the gift shop."

"Stand in front of it," Scott directed.

"Okay, okay. But you better shoot me from behind," Shade said moving to the picture.

"Oh, I'll shoot plenty of your behind."

With a roll of her eyes, Shade turned to strike a pose in front of the painting,

"I am sensing the spirit of the painter..." Shade began, imitating Cookie Daniel's famed melodramatic style. "He suffered greatly in his brief time on this plane from.... Wait, it's coming to me...a total lack of talent."

"You've got that right."

"It's really not *that* bad," she admitted as she gave it a more detailed appraisal. "I like the dark moodiness—reminds me of something by Caspar Friedrich."

She stepped back to take in the whole of the large, unearthly landscape. A writhing desert stretched to merge into a roiling tawny sky, beneath which a desolate tree thrust itself up from the ground like the withered hand of some Egyptian mummy. Dark, mottled crows—fashioned from thick slashes of paint—lifted their heads in hungry anticipation, as if waiting for something to fall from above.

Something is happening, Shade sensed faintly. She felt certain the painting held answers. Unfortunately, it stubbornly refused any attempt to be read. She struggled to fathom its secrets until hot needles of pain burrowed their way into her head, heralding a familiar, but much stronger psychic event.

She didn't have to wait long for the full impact to be felt.

There was a flash of light as a ribbon of undulating colors flowed like a prismatic waterfall. As it passed through her, Shade found herself in an ever-expanding passage that became longer with each step. An argentous glow illuminated the walls and cast shadows of some unseen presence walking alongside her.

Ahead the air rippled like heat waves, forming a reflective surface. Cautiously, she peered into the mirror. She wasn't totally surprised when another face looked back at her.

Lifting a hand, she reached out toward the reflection's dark hair and vivid hazel eyes. The woman in the reflection did likewise. Like a hand dipping into water, the two seemed to meet and fuse briefly.

As they touched, Shade felt electricity course through her body, snapping her head back. Her head was pulled into the silvery surface to glimpse thousands of images rush before her like an impossible kaleidoscope.

The surge of images paused. Shade briefly saw a woman with a sword, but then she was lost again in the roar of color. Breathless, she grasped the sides of the mirror and extricated herself from the silvery pool. Now, only her own pale dream features were reflected.

She heard a faint voice called out: *Beware the Ref-ah-eem!*

As the words echoed away into nothing, Shade sensed an undercurrent of frustration. The apparition seemed desperate and impatient. She glanced once more at the mirror.

If you are trying to tell me something, she thought, cringing from the ache in her temple, *I'm going to need more than that!*

Shade felt the connection with the woman break; with a jolt, she was suddenly back in the hallway, staring at Scott.

"What was it she said?" struggling to remember.

Scott's eyebrows raised in a look of concerned confusion. But Shade didn't notice. Her own brow was furrowed in frustration, as she attempted to recall what so faintly the woman had whispered.

"Remember the Refa—Ref-ah-eem? What the hell is the Ref-ah-eem?"

A scream from the stairwell at the far end of the hall shattered Shade's thoughts.

Looking at each other, faces etched with concern, the pair raced toward the stairs.

31

"You seem to be having more than your share of problems, Mr. Wolf." Sheriff Raney watched in stony silence as Nancy Rand's body was removed by men from the county medical examiner's office.

While the Sheriff's words seemed almost sympathetic, Matt nonetheless sensed an edge of concern—perhaps even an accusation.

"Let's see, this makes...four incidents this week and about nine over the last two months. Anything you want to tell me?"

"Frankly, Sheriff, I can't explain it." Honestly, Matt had no idea how to explain what was happening in a way that wouldn't make him look crazy.

Maybe I am crazy, he thought. *Maybe there are ghosts here and maybe what my grandfather said....* He shook the thought from his head. *That was a mistake. Whatever that had been was a mistake. This was now and very real,* he reminded himself, as he caught a final fleeting glimpse of Nancy's body being carried down the stairs on a stretcher. The guys from the M.E.'s office weren't happy when they learned the elevators were not working.

"Know of anyone who might have reason to sabotage your work here?"

"I can't imagine. This entire community stands to gain from the hotel's restoration."

"And what was she doing right before she fell?"

"Checking the progress on the unfinished floors."

"You talk to her before the fall?"

"Not right before. I was still a few floors below when I saw she was calling my phone. The next thing I know, she...."

Matt saw Jason Williams enter the room and stop abruptly as he took in the scene.

"Do you know if she had family?" The Sheriff asked.

"No." Matt shook his head. "No close family, that is. You will probably want to contact her lawyer back in Chicago. I'll give you his name."

"Well, for now, I think that about does it." The Sheriff nodded to Matt. "I may have some more questions once the medical examiner has submitted his report."

"Thank you, Sheriff," Matt spoke softly before Raney left with a tip of the hat.

"What happened, Matt?" Jason Williams' voice was deep, concerned.

"My boss, Nancy Rand, fell down the stairs. She died."

"Is that what killed her?"

"EMT says so far it looks like her heart went," Matt replied. "She had a history and was on medication for it."

"I'm sorry, Matt." Jason spoke the words absently. He stared blankly, as if searching for something or perhaps visualizing.

"What is it?"

"Where was she? Before the fall, I mean?"

"She'd told one of the workers that she was going to inspect the upper floors. Why?"

"We picked up some readings."

"What kind of readings?"

Jason didn't seem to hear. "Was anybody up there with her?"

"Just the plumbers. They were heading out as it happened."

"What about Skyler's crew?"

"Most of them were elsewhere. Shade and Scott were a few floors below where she fell. They heard her scream." Matt cringed with fresh anguish.

"I understand." Jason offered reassuringly. "I know what it is to stand by helplessly watching someone you care about die."

Matt shrugged, neither accepting nor rejecting the commiseration.

"What were these readings you were talking about?" Matt asked after a long pause, eager to get his mind on anything else for at least a few minutes.

"We picked up anomalies at the same time as we recorded something on the audio."

"Something?" Matt asked, anxiety churning his gut.

"It was muffled, but seemed to be some kind of humming. Carrie confirmed there were no trucks or construction or machinery outside the hotel that would have registered such a frequency. It almost seemed harmonic. I was checking for any electrical interference that might explain it."

"Humming? I never heard anything like that."

"You say you were having the plumbing worked on? That might account for it. Pipes equalizing. I guess we won't know for sure until we clean up the recording."

"Had you heard any of this before?" Matt asked.

"No. We had just finished the setup and were running calibration tests."

"So, it could have been a bug in the system?"

"It probably was," Jason admitted. "We have to check all the possibilities to be sure."

"But you have to admit, it's strange that you get this weird humming sound right when Nancy dies."

"It's a coincidence, Matt." Jason had seen grieving people try to over-complicate a simple matter. Their sheer refusal to accept death left them seeking out mysteries and lingering over questions.

"Show me the readings. If anyone knows this building, it's me. I want to know what caused your anomaly."

"It's just raw data, Wolf: temperature, barometric pressure, ion count... It won't help you solve anything. You're letting this place get to you. Believe me, I've seen it before."

"I know," Matt sighed ruefully. "It's the accidents, the fights, the missing tools and now Nancy. It's hard not to think this place is evil."

"Trust me, Matt. The hotel is not haunted."

"Jason," the walkie-talkie on his belt squawked. "Jason! We have another sensor anomaly—just like before!"

32

"Okay, Cookie, we'll be running a camera over here," Skyler pointed to where a bored Alex stood holding a camera over his shoulder. "As you begin to sense the rooms, we'll just tag along. Don't let us bother you."

"Oh, dear, you won't bother me. Once I begin to read a location, I notice nothing but what the spirits and angels wish to communicate through me."

Skyler glanced sideways at Alex, "Well, perhaps we should begin then."

Cookie walked out into the middle of the hallway and placed a hand to her temple, "I'm sensing…a sadness here. It's important that we all project positive energy. Then we can welcome the dear lost souls with love and light. We will guide them to crossing over, to complete their journey."

God, my head is splitting! I should never have had that third martini on that layover in Dallas. I need food! Just let me get through this…just get me through this….

"Yes…there is a lot of energy here. Spirits! Speak to us! We are your friends."

Cookie began walking down the hall as Skyler and Alex trailed behind. She stopped at a room that had once held supplies for the maids on this floor. However, it was recently designated the catchall for old nursery furniture bound for an antique auction. Whimsical cribs, emblazoned with fairy tale paintings, now filled the small room.

"What are you sensing, Mrs. Daniels?" Skyler noticed that Cookie had fixated on the far corner.

Alex trained the camera on Cookie, as tears welled up in her eyes and her countenance became grief-stricken. "So much loneliness…so young.…"

Composing herself, she continued, "I'm sensing the pitiful soul of a child that has lost his way. Perhaps our love and energy will guide him home." Cookie looked imploringly at Skyler, one performer to another, "Skyler, will you assist me?"

Skyler quickly crossed over to Cookie, making sure her best side always faced the camera. The two stood face to face, holding hands as the camera zoomed in on their awkward clasp.

After a few moments, Cookie lifted her head upward and called out, "My precious lost soul, we are here in peace. Listen to the comfort and love in my voice. Follow it. Let it guide you to whatever warmth and solace you seek. Relinquish your earthbound ties and soar free through the sky, following the sound of love homeward."

The floor shifted beneath them, sending the tiny rocker in Motion while a shower of dust and plaster rained from the ceiling above.

Skyler cried out to Alex as she shook the dust from herself. "Did you get that!?"

"Yeah, I got it," he said, coughing up the plaster dust. "But I don't know what the hell I got!"

"Keep it rolling, Alex. We'll edit later," Skyler commanded before turning back to Cookie. "Mrs. Daniels, you're the expert in these matters. What happened? What did we just witness?"

Cookie, completely confused by what had transpired, could only stare around her at the fallen plaster. She glanced up to the ceiling where tiny spider cracks branched out from the light fixture. This had never happened in the old days when she and her late husband worked the medium circuit. She stammered slowly while her mind raced, seeking something to say.

"Yes. Well. That was certainly interesting. Some-sometimes, spirits become…attached to a place."

"You mean it views this as its home? Does that mean it lived here once?"

"Perhaps. Or it simply became lost, in a manner of speaking. Any familiar place can become a wayward spirit's home. And just as we wouldn't want to be kicked out of ours, these spirits can grow fiercely attached." Cookie was actually rather proud of herself for coming up with that one. "Yes, I think that's what we witnessed. The spirit was angry, fearing we were trying to get rid of it."

"Thank you, Cookie. That was…*interesting*."

Switching off her mic, she turned to Alex. "Let's wrap it there. I think that was a great shot." She brushed away the plaster that seemed to coat her whole body.

The room suddenly reverberated with a metallic moan that had them covering their ears. Like a giant bellows, the ceiling expanded outward, belching a fresh shower of plaster and dust down on the trio.

As they rushed to the door, a ceiling joist fell free, slamming Alex into the wall and knocking the camera from his grip.

"My God!" Skyler screamed. "The video!"

Cookie staggered to where Alex had fallen. Blood gushed down one side of his face and he was unmoving. She bent over him and listened, relieved to hear a heartbeat.

"Get help!" She called to the reporter.

"What?" Skyler snapped as she bent over to pick up another piece of the ruined camera. "We have to have that film! I gotta have it!"

Cookie was astonished. It seemed the stories about Skyler were true: she *was* a careerist bitch!

But to be so cold....

"He's hurt badly!" Cookie screamed. "My God, call for help!"

33

While the strange incident had left her shaken, Cookie Daniels was also secretly thrilled. Maybe her recent slump would soon come to an end. No one these days seemed to remember she had once been the 'Psychic to the Stars'. Appearances on *Carson*, *Good Morning America*, and even visits to the White House flashed through her mind. Perhaps with this gig, she could reclaim her crown.

Cookie stepped off the landing to what she assumed was her floor. However, she noted with a bit of frustration that she had no clue which floor she was on.

How many stairs did I climb, anyway, she wondered.

This floor looked different than hers. She remembered freshly laid soft blue and gold carpet. This floor, however, had a different color scheme. An old-fashioned Persian runner, in maroon and navy, ran the length of a long corridor. The hall seemed darker, too. In fact, she swore that at....

Abruptly, a low, rhythmic sound emerged from one of the rooms further ahead.

Several wary strides later, Cookie had located the room from which the strange noise issued. Placing her ear tentatively to the door, she heard the sounds clarify into a soft keening, like a sulking child in the last stages of a tantrum. It was a sorrowful tattoo repeated over and over.

She tried to remember who she had seen downstairs, tried to figure out if any had been missing. Was someone sick? Had someone been hurt?

"Hello! Are you all right?" she called out, knocking softly on the door.

The noise ceased.

Slowly, she grasped the knob and turned gently. As the door widened with a screech, she peeked in.

"Hello!" She called again. "It's Cookie Daniels. Are you all right?"

As her eyes adjusted to the dimness, she could see that the room was empty. Where did they go? She knew with certainty that she hadn't imagined it. She had clearly heard soft moans.

Something about the room seemed wrong. Cookie peered about, searching for the reason. *Odd,* she thought, *this room looks as it must have decades ago.* The furnishings, the carpet, and the thick brocade curtains framing the windows all wore a heavy mantle of disuse and neglect.

A ragged sigh turned her gaze toward the bed once more. Straining intently to peer into the gloom, Cookie stumbled in shock as she witnessed a pale, pearlescent glow budding near the bed.

She watched, awe-struck, as it began to stretch and grow into an indistinct, but nonetheless human shape. As another whimper echoed in the still air, the shape began to take on nascent features. She—for the figure emerging from that translucent mist was distinctly feminine—looked to be a woman of about twenty. With her short, bobbed hair Cookie was reminded of some tragic Fitzgeraldian heroine.

The woman's face slowly rotated to meet Cookie's. One whole side was a maze of cuts and bruises.

Filling with a dread that set into her limbs like a sticky mass, Cookie wobbled wordlessly backwards. She bumped into the dresser, knocking free a small vase that shattered softly into several pieces upon the carpet.

After the initial shock, Cookie calmed some. She took a better look at the woman and felt a strange pang of empathy. She had seen cut lips and swollen eyes like that before among some of her clients, women who had chosen to let the wrong kind of man into their lives.

The woman raised her desperate eyes to Cookie's own, struggling to speak.

"The storm..." she breathed at last in a dry sound like the whisper of wind-blown autumn leaves.

A new tension in the figure on the bed drew Cookie's eyes toward the door where a male figure now stood. Cookie drew in a sharp breath. He was barely visible, not as clear as the woman on the bed.

The two entities were alike and yet dissimilar. While the woman existed in a glow of faint pastels, the man was a dingy gray hue, which gave off waves of icy anger. The air grew frosty in his presence and Cookie sidled fearfully against the wall. The woman's whimpers and moans began again as the dark presence filled the room. Within seconds, he had totally consumed the frail, battered woman. Then suddenly, they were both gone.

Cookie stared at the empty bed for limitless seconds before bolting to the door. Racing down the hall, she urgently sought the familiarity of the blue and gold carpet. In the distance, she could hear the wind quicken. As she raced past a bank of windows, she spotted a cold line of clouds blooming in the west and she heard the basso rumble of approaching thunder.

35

A jagged streak of lightning tore across the sky. The weather forecast had mentioned scattered thunderstorms, but the fierce clouds overhead hinted at worse.

Karen checked her reflection one last time, and with a bracing sigh, opened the ancient bronze door to the hotel. She was grateful for Matt's invitation. With the dig shut down, she had little else to do on a stormy night in Corvus Mound.

As she entered the foyer, she made sure the carryall on her shoulder was secure. She decided to take the sword home with her as she left work, but didn't want to leave it in the car. *It was probably somebody's sick idea of a joke*, she thought. *But better safe than sorry, as they say.*

Nervously smoothing the front of her slacks, she crossed the entry and stepped down into the lobby.

It was a pleasing shock to see the hotel so elegantly appointed. Matt had a gift all right. However, in contrast to the opulently restored lobby, those gathered therein were a disparate, rag-tag group, awash in the trappings of modern life.

One entire corner was filled with an assortment of electronic equipment being fussed over by an anxious-looking young man who fidgeted nervously as he typed away at his laptop. A young woman in glasses, working nearby, shot him an exasperated look before folding her laptop and fleeing to a sofa some feet away.

At one of the windows, an older woman stood in a pale pink dress, disaffectedly fussing with a huge crystal hanging from her neck. Slouching in an armchair was a young woman in black, tugging a spiked dog collar at her neck, a look of carefully feigned boredom on her pale face. Her eyes, Karen decided, were too...*watchful* for someone truly disinterested.

Amid a clutter of lighting equipment and cameras stood the newswoman, Skyler Dunworth-Michaels, fashionably—if not overly—dressed in heels and a navy silk suit. She was speaking heatedly to Matt and a tall black man.

Several other people stood clustered in the background, but before she could do more than glance at them, Matt spotted her and quickly strode forward.

"You made it!" he exclaimed, reaching out to take her hand. He led her into the group, making introductions as they walked.

During a brief pause following the introductions, Karen softly conveyed her sympathies at Nancy Rand's death.

"How did you find out?" Matt asked in surprise.

"Small town," she explained. "They don't have much else to talk about."

"Of course they don't," Matt said sourly. "To make matters worse, one of the cameramen was injured pretty badly."

"My God," Karen sighed. "Will he be alright?"

"We don't know yet. Richard, one of the guests, drove him to the hospital."

"I'm sorry, Matt." Karen knew it was a hollow offering, but she simply didn't know what to say.

The pair drifted to the expansive marble registration desk where several chafing dishes and a makeshift bar had been set up.

"Well, if you need someone to talk to...." Karen let the sentiment trail. She could see he was shutting down some. *Don't push, Karen.*

"Wine?" he asked.

"Oh, yes," she replied, gratefully taking the proffered glass.

Karen had just started to take a much needed sip, when the older woman at the window turned to her.

"You've been here before." Devoid of expression, the words came out a statement rather than a question.

"Once, as a child. My aunt took me."

The woman nodded, as if she had expected that response, and then turned back to the window.

"That was about three years before the hotel closed," Karen continued as she turned back to Matt.

"I bet it was really lovely back then," a soft voice sighed from near the fireplace. Karen turned in time to catch a wistful smile fade from the lips of the shy girl introduced earlier as Carrie. Her furtive eyes encompassed the room in dreamy admiration.

"What do you mean 'back then'?" Matt asked in mock severity. "We've been working like Trojans just to get this place ready. The rest of the hotel may still look like a disaster, but this lobby down-right rocks, thank you very much!"

"S-sorry." Carrie stammered. "I—I just meant when it was...it was open and had lots of people running around in it. You know, more full of life."

Karen noticed how Matt's disarming smile had the near-magical effect of quelling the girl's discomfort and embarrassment. She wondered for a moment if all his flirtations were not perhaps some manipulation. But she quickly reprimanded herself for indulging such paranoia.

That was the past, remember?

"There's a storm coming," the woman at the window intoned matter-of-factly without taking her eyes off the gathering dark outside. In support of her assertion, a peel of thunder broke in the distance.

"You mentioned that before, Cookie," Skyler stated with an annoyed tone. "The meteorologist at the station says any bad storms will totally miss us."

"It's coming, all right." The woman in pink stated flatly.

Karen shivered at the sound of that strangely inflectionless voice. There had been no hint of emotion at all in that short statement. It had the mechanical tones of a prerecorded time and temperature message. She dragged her eyes away from the woman and found herself being watched by the young lady Matt introduced as Shade.

"Anyway, I think you did a great job." Karen assured Matt.

Conversations, a little louder than necessary began springing up around the room, as if the others were trying to drown out the woman in pink. Yet, she wasn't totally forgotten. In the midst of a conversation, Karen would see someone steal a glance toward the window where the woman stood sentinel. *Maybe the death of Matt's boss had affected her*, Karen thought. That would definitely explain her strange behavior and everyone's concern. *Such a tragedy and so close to the hotel's grand opening.*

"Karen is an archaeologist working at the mounds," Matt announced to the group. "Tell us about the hotel," he urged, inviting her to take a seat. The distraction worked and the others found themselves clustering around, listening to the story of the building.

"Well, I don't remember too much. I was just a kid."

"What do you remember best?" Carrie asked.

"Oddly, the smell of the lemon oil they used to polish the woodwork. Isn't that strange?"

"Sense memories are among the most powerful and are often triggered by smells. Is that 'scientific' enough for you, Jason?"

It took Karen several long seconds to realize just who had spoken. When she realized it was Shade, Karen noted it was the first time she heard the young woman speak.

There was an undercurrent in the room, she observed. She felt like she had walked into a movie too late, having missed the crucial plot point. Shade, Jason, and Cookie formed a triangle of tension in the room.

"Like smelling a perfume and remembering somebody?" Carrie asked. "Whenever I smell *Tabu*, I always think of my grandmother. It was her favorite."

"Well, the smell of that food is reminding me I'm starved!" the remaining cameraman quipped.

There was a small ripple of laughter throughout the group as they all grasped eagerly at the small joke. Soon, the normal level of chatter resumed and several guests wandered over to examine the buffet.

Karen looked back to the window where the woman in pink still stood, staring into the dark. For a moment the drawn, almost haggard planes of her face were illuminated by the storm. In a flash of lightning, the beast from her dream pawed at the glass, hunting for a weakness.

With a start, Karen gasped, overwhelmed by a sudden desire to leave. Another shudder of light outside drew her gaze involuntarily back to where Cookie stood. There was nothing in the window except the darkness and a reflection of the sad woman in pink.

What is wrong with me, she wondered in alarm. She had the strangest desire to run from the building and not stop until she was miles away.

Then the welts on her hand returned.

35

The aroma of the food triggered a growling in Shade. It had been late the night before since she had anything real to eat. That gas station bag of Doritos hardly counted, she decided. She eyed the selections on the buffet: an assortment of southern-friend victuals from chicken to okra. While not an overly-conscientious eater, Shade nonetheless was hesitant to dive headlong into a vat of grease. Then she spied it, a tempting piece of grilled chicken breast calling her name.

"Isn't it amazing how a little food can make you feel so much more human?" a voice spoke from behind. Shade turned to find the mousy brunette from William's team pushing her glasses back up the bridge of her nose.

"You're the video expert with Williams, aren't you?"

"Carrie Pierce." The girl nearly toppled her plate as she juggled to extend a hand. "I'm the team's imaging specialist. I do the photos, video… You name it, I do it."

"Can I have that in writing," Scott asked lasciviously as he interrupted to grab a roll off the tray beside them. "You know, for future reference? I've been thinking of expanding my horizons," he told her with a leer.

"That's not what I meant," She actually turned red as he mouthed a kiss toward her.

"Maybe you need your horizons expanded, too?"

"I don't think adding porn auteur to your resume quite amounts to an expanded horizon," Shade spoke coolly while spearing the piece of chicken onto her plate.

She felt a pang of pity watching the young ingénue parry Scott's aggressive flirtations with little success. But Shade was hungry and couldn't rescue Carrie all night. So, dismissing herself from the conversation, she walked back to the leather sofa parked in front of the large flickering fireplace.

Carrie managed to halt her awkward encounter a few moments later and sat herself on the stone hearth opposite Shade.

"Do you mind?" The woman asked timidly.

"Knock yourself out," Shade replied noncommittally.

The girl returned a small smile and then cocked her head curiously, like a bird. Something on the far wall suddenly caught her attention.

"What is it?" Scott asked, as he grabbed a seat alongside the two women.

"Did you notice how many crows there are in this place?" Carrie asked. She indicated a strange and intricate carving in the mahogany paneling along the far wall.

"Where? Where?" He intoned with mock fear as he pointed to his naked head. "Look, folks, I need to know these things!"

Carrie laughed softly as she pointed out both the carving and a framed painting behind the check-in counter.

"There are at least two other paintings with crows upstairs," she added.

"Yeah, Shade and I saw one," Scott said. "There is also a butt ugly carving over the door."

"*That* I had noticed," Shade murmured. She flexed her hand as the stinging pain from her dream returned.

There were so many things to notice in this place. Distraction was sometimes a real danger. She had been on sensory overload for quite a while now. Shade knew that a burnout was coming if this didn't let up soon.

She was not the only one receiving. Shade sensed something about the new woman, Karen. *She's not psychic—not really*, Shade decided after a moment. *Maybe it's just this place, but she is definitely switched on right now. I wonder if she's the one the dream chick told me to help.*

The change she witnessed in Cookie earlier also had been...interesting. Shade felt certain this hotel was supplying a lot of psychic energy. And it wasn't a great leap in logic to conclude it was beginning to affect its occupants. Whereas before, Cookie would have been lucky to guess her own age, she was now receiving many of the same impressions Shade was sensing.

A voice from behind the group brought her out of her thoughts.

"The name should have warned you, people," Peter Evans, called from his nest of electronics. He spun in his chair to face them with a self-satisfied grin.

"The name?" Scott looked confused

"What are you talking about?" Carrie asked.

"*Corvus* Mound." He emphasized the word with a pedantic lilt. "I am surrounded by the intellectually inferior. How am I to survive? *Corvus*. It's Latin for crow."

"*Corvus brachyrhynchos*" Shade stated absently as she focused on the mantel's strangely melancholic carving.

"Yes...." Peter gave her a wary look.

"Ah-ha!" Jason piped in as he approached the cluster of people. "An equal at last. I guess you're finally saved from the vile philistines you've been forced to associate with!"

"Yes." Peter shot Jason an irritated look. "That's the term used for both ravens and crows."

"How did you know?" Scott queried.

"Research." He pulled a skinny paperback book from his pocket and slapped it on the table. On the cover was a crude drawing of a crow sitting on a hill under the title *History of Corvus Mound*. "They were selling these over at the drugstore. They have a souvenir area at the front with postcards and stuff."

"You're joking?" Carrie peered over her greasy frames.

"About the crows?"

"No, about the souvenirs," she responded. "A gift shop for a town like this?"

"You can go shopping later," Scott interrupted dismissively. "What else does it say?"

"The usual stuff about the founding families and, what fruit trees they planted, and a bunch of boring crap like that. Of course, there's the requisite chapter on all the firsts: church, school, crackhouse." Then, after an impactful pause, he added, "Then there's the hotel."

"Good stuff?" Scott begged, eagerly hitching his chair a little closer.

"Deaths, scandals, ghosts...." Peter's voice was rich with disdain and he tugged at his collar as if it had grown tight.

"Do tell us all about it!" Scott urged, impersonating excited schoolgirl.

"Come on, guys!" Carrie demanded. "You don't believe that stuff do you?

"Maybe...." Scott drawled sheepishly. "Come on, man, tell us some more."

Others in the room had stopped to listen to the conversation. Shade sensed that what obviously began as a clever way to boast of his intellectual prowess had suddenly become tiresome for Peter. She could tell the young man had an elevated sense of self-importance.

"Ms. Houston," Peter spoke up, drawing the archaeologist into the mix. "You probably know a lot more about the hotel than this book does."

All eyes turned expectantly toward Karen, who now found herself the center of attention.

"Give us the dirt," Scott begged.

"Okay...." Karen began hesitantly. "Well, during one a party in the twenties, a woman was found dancing naked in the garden pond." Karen smiled at their faces. "Pretty tame by today's standards, but quite a scandal then."

"The paparazzi wouldn't give it a second glance," Scott agreed.

"And," she continued, "ballot boxes from the years the hotel served as a polling station were frequently found padded with names from a nearby cemetery."

"What about the ghosts?" Shade asked quietly. "What do you know about those stories?"

"Over the years, there have been reports of people seeing things: shadowy figures, a lady in white...all the usual stuff, I guess."

"So, what's with all the crows?" Scott asked.

"Local legend says there have always been large numbers of crows here. Early explorers even noted it and named the mounds after them, according to one legend."

"So, they're like the town symbol?" Carrie asked. "Isn't there an old nursery rhyme or something, 'one crow for luck...'?"

"I think it depends on how many there are," Shade said as she pulled out her NetFone for reference.

"What's that? Your personal library?" Scott quipped.

"Pretty much. 'Knowledge is power,' my friend. Anyway, one crow is actually unlucky according to most sources. However, two through five: it's all good. Six or more...." Looking up from the screen, "Well, I'll be avoiding any murders of crows in the future."

"But the Native Americans saw them as good spirits, didn't they?" Matt asked.

"Some do, but many see them as tricksters," Shade said.

"Yes," Karen interjected as she walked to where she could see the carving more clearly. "Several tribes viewed them as shapeshifters, made of shadow and possessing the ability to change shape at will. Moreover, crows are scavengers, which associates them with death. In fact, even today, we don't call it a flock of crows; it's a *murder*."

"That kinship with darkness and death is why they're viewed as emissaries of the underworld," Shade added.

Before the echo of her words had fully died in the expanse of the lobby, shade looked down at her hand. It was burning again. When she looked up, she caught site of Karen, cradling the same hand with a pained expression. *Does she have the welts too?*

"Well, on that cheerful note," Scott declared sarcastically, "I need something to eat. Anyone else want to see what's for dessert?"

Several of the group, still chuckling, turned away to follow Scott when a sudden beeping blared from the equipment in the far corner.

Peter and Carrie dashed to their stations, leaping over the chairs in the process. As Jason's team busily worked, the others simply stared in mounting incomprehension.

"I've got movement on the fourth floor!" Peter cried hoarsely. "Thermals are tripping all over the place!"

36

What is it?" Skyler asked as she raced back to rejoin the group. The others ignored her, instead concentrating on their equipment and calling out incomprehensible readings.

She snapped at Scott, directing him to his camera.

"Temperature variance on the second and third floors," Evans called out over the general din. "Negative twenty from the mean!"

The tension in the man was clearly visible as he moved in rapid, jerky movements. He snarled at Scott when the cameraman got in his way.

"Are we recording?" Jason shouted, watching the oscilloscope dance up and down with dizzying speed. He grabbed an equipment belt, strapped it on, and scanned the other monitors.

Shade felt a familiar tingle along her nerves; a feather-light touch that set her hair bristling and her heart pounding. Struggling to her feet, she saw the crows on the far wall and remembered the stream of black that tore past her in Seattle.

Omens, she thought bitterly. *Damn it!* From deep beneath them, she sensed something rising rapidly upward, surging like a geyser from the dark heart of the earth. The impression was immense, sinister, and very, very powerful.

"Electromagnetic fields are going crazy!" Peter cried, tossing Jason a two-way radio. "Motion sensors are going off, too. It's sporadic. I—I can't localize anything!"

"What's the reading?" Catching the radio in his hand, Jason fastened a monitor in one ear.

"It's coming fast!" Shade cried, her eyes wild and chest suddenly heaving. A harsh cry was torn from her just as all hell broke loose around them. "Now!"

A blast of air charged through the building, bursting open doors, toppling vases, and knocking over chairs. The floor beneath buckled and heaved. Chandeliers swayed and danced as light bulbs exploded, sending out fierce showers of sparks.

Slamming people to the floor, the force sped heedlessly throughout the rooms. All around, people struggled to their feet. Their cries filled the air as they began wildly searching the room for an exit.

"Earthquake!"

"In Oklahoma?!"

"Impossible—get me readings!"

"Run!"

A powerful onslaught of images shot through Shade like blooming starbursts in her head. She recoiled, staggering as they pounded her physically. She felt her neck jerk painfully and her back arch, as if something had her in its grasp.

In her mind, Shade saw herself as a woman running with long powerful strides and heard the anguished cry. She raised a sword as shadowy black crows took flight. Gathering together they lashed out at the woman, pummeled her into the hard ground as the earth shook ferociously.

There seemed to be copies of her; woman after woman after woman stretching back through infinity. She felt something crawling beneath her skin, sinking deep into flesh, into the marrow of her bones...

Suddenly, Shade saw a withered, wizened man lift high a vessel—the vessel of Ra-may, though she had no idea how she knew this—and heard him utter: "hilka, hilka...."

But as the man spoke, a deadly hum began building in the—

"The basement!" Shade screamed in agony as a final tendril of this dark psychic energy lashed out at her exhausted mind. Seconds later, she crumpled to the floor.

A chorus of clicks filled the hotel as the security doors automatically locked. The lights flickered and dimmed briefly before plunging the hotel into total darkness.

Suddenly, all was pandemonium. Everyone began talking at once. Frantic shouts merged with hysterical sobs in an indistinguishable cacophony, above which only one sound pierced the din.

From her perch by the window, Cookie laughed. She laughed with the delighted fervor of a woman gone completely mad.

37

"Shut up!" Jason barked at Cookie. Her shrill laughter stopped abruptly.

"Please, tell me we got something, anything?" Skyler begged.

"Not now, Skyler!" Scott shouted as he raced to where Shade lay still on the floor.

"Calm down," Matt's voice boomed over the commotion. "In a minute, the power will kick back on."

"Matt!" Scott called out from windows by the main doors. "We're the only ones without electricity. The rest of the town is lit up."

"Did the backups kick in?" Jason asked his team as he began checking his equipment. "Prime the generator! I don't want to lose what we're getting here."

"My God!" Peter finally blurted out, once he composed himself. "This can't be...." There was a strange, wild look to him and he began to shake with uncontrollable excitement. "This is crazy. It's impossible!"

"What?" Jason demanded.

"That...*event* tripped sensors all over the building!" His fingers continued flying over the keyboard, reading screen after screen. "I've got the Fourth of July going on here! Heat, motion, infrasonics...the whole enchilada!"

"I've got images!" Carrie blurted without even raising her head from the monitors. "But nothing else!"

"Jason!" Matt shouted. "Help us get Shade to the couch!"

"Check the UV cams!" Jason directed, as he raced to help Matt.

"Careful, she may be in shock!" Scott told them, as the three men lifted Shade's still form.

"Should we move her?" Skyler asked. Litigation and lawsuits were just what she needed. First Alex and now this. She knew she could buy off the cameraman, but that Hoffmeyer woman was a mystery. "If she's hurt... I mean, she might sue."

"We can't leave her on the floor!" Matt snapped, glancing around the demolished room.

"Caring to the end," Jason muttered.

"What the hell happened!?" Skyler focused on Matt.

It was his damn hotel. Things were moving too fast and she was losing control of the group. Her skin felt hot, too tight, and her head was aching.

"I demand some answers!"

Ignoring her, Scott yelled out, "Somebody get a towel, some water."

Cookie, regaining some of her old self, dashed to the buffet table and snatched a pitcher of water and a handful of cloth napkins.

Karen looked around the room, desperate for a blanket, a towel, something to keep Shade warm. Suddenly, she spotted a small gift shop tucked among the shadows in the far corner. She dashed inside, instantly noticing a box of embroidered robes. She grabbed one and raced back to where Matt had placed Shade on one of the longer sofas.

Shade began to mumble, "The basement.... The basement...."

"She's delirious!" Matt called out with growing dread.

"It doesn't look like she hit her head when she fell," Scott assured. "She's probably just dazed."

The cameraman dampened the napkins with the water from the pitcher and laid the compress across Shade's forehead. He checked her pulse again.

"Pulse is slow but steady".

"Is she okay?" Jason asked with deep concern as he returned to the group.

"The basement?" Matt repeated softly. "She said that earlier, before she collapsed. I don't know what she means, but I'd better go check that out. You guys stay here."

"I'm going with you," Jason said. "Guys, watch the monitors!"

38

The two men rapidly followed the dark corridors that led from the lobby, through the offices, and toward the back stairs.

Below grade, lay the sprawling warren of rooms comprising the kitchen, laundry, housekeeping and storage facilities. Something crashed in the darkness below, at the far limit of the emergency lights.

"Jason!" Matt urged in a strained whisper. "Did you hear that? Someone's down there."

Jason's training as a police officer instinctively kicked in. Adopting a defensive stance, he slowly descended into the void.

"Damn!" he cried. "It's pitch black down there. Got any flashlights?"

Matt worked his way over to a nearby closet and returned moments later with a pair of flashlights. He stepped forward, sweeping the stairs with the dim amber beam.

Here we go, he thought.

Once they reached the bottom, Jason and Matt spread out to search the maze of halls and rooms.

A few moments later, Jason hissed across the darkness, "Listen!"

From somewhere off to the right, Matt heard a faint moan. As his eyes grew accustomed to the feeble light, he detected a subtle glow emanating from the far end of the hall.

Following it to its source, Matt discovered the illumination came from within the same pit from which they had pulled the city inspector earlier.

"This place is a maze!" Jason whispered as he caught up with Matt. "What's in there?"

"That's the original water well. Sealed up decades ago."

Cautiously moving forward, the two crawled inside the hole of damaged plaster and crept softly to the rim of the old well. Hesitantly, the two peered down its throat.

"Not very deep," Jason remarked.

"I think they must have back-filled it," Matt spoke quietly.

In the sickly glow of an old camping lantern, the two spotted a man laying face down on the floor, apparently unconscious. In one hand, he held a clay flask; similar to the one Matt's grandfather had given him.

"That must have fallen on him." Jason said, pointing to a large chunk of rock near the man's head.

The stranger moaned and struggled to rise.

"Well, at least he's alive," Matt noted.

"We should get down there," Jason said, pointing to the rope ladder slung over the side.

Within seconds, the two men had descended the ten-foot drop to reach the stranger's supine form.

"Take it easy, fellow. Take it easy." Matt turned him over and saw, with a shock, the ashen face of his grandfather.

"Grandpa... Oh, God! What the hell?"

Matt reached frantically for a pulse and took a deep relieved breath when he felt a faint but steady beat.

As Matt looked to the man's wounds, the cop in Jason automatically began panning his own light around the chamber. Old habits again, he realized, as he assessed the scene. He could just make out, underneath the stale underground odors, a faint but familiar scent.

Old death.

Jason panned his light over something that poked up from the hard packed dirt a few feet away. In the shadows that danced from the old lantern, he could see several skulls grinning in macabre satisfaction.

Jason nodded to the man on the ground by Matt. "So who's our burglar? You seem to know him."

"I haven't stolen anything since I was in the third grade," said the old man.

"That's what they all say, isn't it," Jason pointed out. "Who are you?"

"When it rains it pours...." Matt said with sigh of exhaustion. "Jason, meet my grandfather: Ben Yellow Wolf."

Jason glanced at Matt for a long moment and then looked at the older man seeking some resemblance. The older man tried to get up but gasped as his leg collapsed under him.

"I'm okay." He told the other two when they reached out to support him. "Just strained my leg a bit when I fell and then that rock hit me when the earth shook."

"All right, then, Mr. Yellow Wolf. Come on," Jason said, reaching down to help hoist the man to his feet, "let's get out of here."

Abruptly, the air around them changed.

Matt shivered fiercely, noticing a low hum that grew from everywhere at once. It sounded similar to high-voltage machinery, but harsher, more intense. Matt twisted around, trying to locate its source.

His grandfather began to shakily move toward the opening.

"If you don't want to end up like these bones," the old man urged, "you'd better move your asses now!"

Matt, hearing the intensity of the hum escalating with renewed vigor, took one last look around. Somehow, what he had experienced on his grandfather's porch was now coming true. Well, the humming part at least. He still didn't buy it all.

"Williams, I think he's right. We'd better move it!"

Half-supporting and half-dragging the old man up the rope ladder, the trio hurried back toward the stairs at a trot. Behind them, Matt felt something moving, gathering itself. The image of a snake, coiled to strike, sprang to mind.

"Come on!" Matt spurred them faster toward the steps, grunting harshly as he grabbed Yellow Wolf's other side.

He and Jason pushed the man up the stairs as quickly as they dared. Each step fell more urgently than the last, as they raced through the dark labyrinth.

As the men burst back into the lobby, the others rushed forward, all speaking at once.

"Jason! You gotta see these readings!" Carrie called out when she saw him.

Jason released Yellow Wolf to Scott and hurried to the bank of computers. Peter and Carrie nervously eyed the new arrival.

"No time for that now, guys." Jason said as he glimpsed the newest data. "Peter, you and Carrie and see if you can get the lights back on."

Jason began checking some of the monitors, the sound of that hum downstairs still buzzing in his ears. "We need something more than these emergency lights."

As Matt and Scott led Ben to the sofa opposite Shade, she took a good look at the new arrival. His wizened countenance was deeply tanned and scored by countless wrinkles that carved his face into the familiar roadmap of a life long-lived. From beneath his gray mane, a rivulet of blood and sweat traced a path down one grimy cheek.

There was no doubt in her mind. This was the man from the vision.

"What the hell were you doing down there?" Matt demanded. "You crazy old fool! You could have been killed!"

"You wouldn't believe me, so it's probably best if I don't say anything."

"No, that won't cut it! You were trespassing. Are you responsible for all of this?"

"If you believed that, you'd be calling the police right now," Yellow Wolf challenged weakly. "You *know* what caused this."

"Don't bring up that bullshit now," Matt snapped angrily. "I should have taken you to your sister's after all. But now, you can just try explaining that story to the police."

Karen turned to Matt, "Who is he?"

"Everybody," Matt said, turning to the others. "Meet my grandfather, Ben Yellow Wolf."

"Your grandfather?" Skyler asked with interest. "What's he doing here?"

"Breaking and entering. Trespassing. Theft, for all I know!"

"You're not going to call the police on your own grandfather, are you Matt?" Cookie wore a pained, maternal expression.

"No," Karen interjected strongly. "He won't because he knows that this," she indicated the devastation around them, "was not caused by an old man."

"I am not that old!" Ben cried out hoarsely as he sat up on the couch.

"Okay, this was not caused by any person here." Karen restated. She took a seat beside the old man and began to clean the wounds on his face. "I can't say what caused all this, but it wasn't the work of an octogenarian."

"I don't know anything anymore." Matt ran a hand through his hair in frustration before turning away. "That's the problem."

"Matt," Shade called out in a tired voice. "Some people here will say this was all a trick."

She slowly drew out fragmented thoughts, trying to make sense of them.

"They claim that there is no such thing as the paranormal. Most of the time that's probably true," she thought of Cookie. "But sometimes there are people like me."

"What do you mean?" Karen asked.

Shade shook her head and then winced in pain. "Tonight, right before that... force blew through, I saw your grandfather in the basement."

"What do you mean you saw me?"

"Then I saw a lot of other things."

"Yeah, I'm sure you did," Jason commented as he joined the group. "That generally happens when you become delirious."

Shade knew the only way to convince Jason was to dredge up what she knew about his wife. As much as she might enjoy sparring with the man, she didn't really want to hurt him. Not if some other way might work.

"Do you know when I first knew I had unusual abilities?"

"Shade, you took a hard fall when you collapsed," Cookie urged. "Rest."

"I was ten when a boy in my town went missing. Everyone was looking for him. Posters went up all over town. No one knew if he was lost, hurt, or even kidnapped."

Her voice, taut with raw emotion and authority, caught their attention. Shade stared into Jason's eyes, challenging him to comprehend.

"But I knew. I woke up in the middle of the night, gasping for breath, clawing at my covers. Terrified. I knew where he was, but not clearly enough to find him. I could only see vague images of places that meant nothing to me."

"The worst part was trying to convince people that what I experienced was real. Finally, after days of trying to convince them, I just blurted out what I had seen: John Deere has seventy-five cents." Even now, it was hard to dredge up those days. "It made no sense, and more than a few looked at me like I was crazy—including my parents.

A few weeks later, though, his body was found in an abandoned gas station outside town. He had fallen inside an old oil tank."

"How awful." Karen whispered.

"Later, I learned that from a small rupture in the tank, you could see an old John Deere sign that read: seventy-five cents a gallon"

"So, John Deere really did have seventy-five cents." Scott murmured as he glanced at Shade with a new respect.

"You said you saw my grandfather?" Matt asked, bringing their eyes back to him.

"Yes. He was holding the vessel of…" She paused, trying to remember. "Ra-may. He was saying things…strange words. They didn't make sense."

"How did you know about that?" Matt asked. "I only found out myself a few days ago."

"Found out what?" Jason asked.

"What he's trying to say," Yellow Wolf added ruefully. "is he's the last in a long line of guardians."

Matt sat down by his grandfather.

"Guardians?" Shade asked, leaning closer. "Guardians of what?"

"Did you have something to do with what happened here tonight?" Jason asked quietly.

"No! Of course, not. I was trying to—"

"You were trying to guard against something here tonight," Shade suggested. "You were trying to stop what happened."

"What the hell are you talking about?" the journalist demanded. "Do we really have time for this? If this fiasco has ruined my chances, I will have your hide, Wolf! We still have video to record. Don't forget."

Scott reared up angrily. He wanted to get in Skyler's face and empty his entire lexicon of four-letter-words. Instead, he stalked to the check-in desk to retrieve his camera.

"The show must go on, right? Come on, boss. Let's go shoot some ghosts."

Before Skyler could frame a retort, Scott grabbed her by the arm and led her forcibly up the broad staircase.

"Bless him," muttered Cookie as she watched the pair disappear into the shadowy realm above. "I may have been saved from committing murder."

"He's in my debt," Jason agreed. "Okay, spill it. What's going on?"

Matt glanced nervously at his grandfather. After a long, reluctant pause, he finally gave the old man a slow nod.

"Tell them," he said. "Tell them what you told me on the porch the other day."

Yellow Wolf struggled to sit up, shrugging off Karen's offer to help. This was something he had waited a long time to say.

A scream shot through the corridors, raw and filled with terror.

"What was that?" Karen asked.

"Carrie!" Jason shouted, already dashing toward the corridor.

39

"Hold that light still!" Peter growled, as he nursed his knee. Fumbling in the dark, he had tripped over something that sent him flying face first into the hard floor of the utility room.

"Fix the lights! Just who did he think he—"

Peter was still pissed at Jason for sending him on what amounted to grunt work.

Carrie tried her best to ignore him. She was more concerned with locating the fuse box and getting these lights back on.

"Can you believe this shit? We finally get the opportunity to evaluate a truly unexplainable event, and he sends us off to find the goddamn light switch!"

"He's our boss," Carrie chided. "The guy who cuts the checks, remember?"

The deeper they went into the hotel's subterranean depths, the further the emergency lights were spaced. The two had spent the last fifteen minutes rooting around in one of the darkest areas with nothing to show for their efforts but bruises.

If he doesn't stop griping, I'm going to give him more than a bruise, she thought, hefting the flashlight.

Carrie readjusted its beam so that it shone directly ahead of Peter while he tried to locate the breaker. She eyed him warily, as he muttered yet another curse.

He was definitely acting strange—stranger than usual anyway. His typically keyed-up nerves had been slowly taken over by an irascible twitch. Always lacking social skills, Peter had become just plain short-tempered and nasty over the last half-hour.

"Can't you hold that damn light steady?"

"I'm holding it fine," Carrie snapped back defensively. "You're the one that can't seem to walk straight!"

"You stupid bi—"

Carrie's look quickly stopped him. Turning away, he continued to mutter garbled obscenities and shoot vicious looks her direction.

She couldn't understand what was happening to him. They had worked together for over a year now, and in all that time, she had never felt threatened. Still, as much as she tried to rationalize the situation, Carrie maintained her distance.

The light in her hand coughed twice, dimmed, and then vanished.

Crap! She thought as the service hall went dark. She slapped the flashlight in desperate hope the beam would return.

"You are absolutely no good to me!" Peter screamed to her from out of the black.

There was a rush of air as Peter's hot breath was suddenly in her face, his claw-like hands clutching her throat.

"Peter!" She croaked, pulling frantically at his hands.

"They're never any damn good to me!" The voice came out harshly as he shoved her into the wall. It was Peter's voice, yet it wasn't. It seemed as if someone else were using it.

The dark became palpable, thick and alive; probing her as she struggled in his grasp. A low sound, like the buzzing of a thousand flies, spilled over her.

The blackness around her stirred. She sensed tentacles twisting themselves around her: lifting her hair, brushing her check, touching her legs. Carrie gasped for breath as she felt this living darkness envelop her.

"No!" she cried as a sudden spasm of terror gave her the strength to ram her knee into Peter's crotch. As she felt his grip on her throat weaken, she flung herself free.

Carrie rushed off into the dark corridor, fumbling blindly. Her head pounded and her lungs burned, but she continued, heedless of the obstacles in her path. Behind her, she could hear Peter screaming strident curses.

"Come back here, bitch!"

"Peter!" she sobbed. "Please, stop doing this!"

"They always talk back!"

She suddenly felt a sharp pain slam into her leg, sending her stumbling to her knees.

"My leg!" Carrie forced herself up and staggered toward the stairs. She heard Peter's footsteps growing louder, closer.

"Somebody, help me!" she screamed, pulling herself up the steps.

"Noooo caaannnn dooo..." Peter's sinister voice sang out from down the hall.

"Help!" she screamed as she reached the top of the stairs.

In horror, she felt Peter pawing at her blouse, roughly grabbing her breasts to pull her back into the darkness below.

Suddenly, the door burst open.

"What the hell?" Jason reached down and dragged Carrie bodily up the last few steps where she slid across the floor.

"Call for help!" he commanded, before turning to her assailant. "Peter, what the—"

With a wordless growl, Peter dove at Jason, sending both tumbling into the abyss. They hit the hard floor with a sick thud.

Before he had time to react, Jason felt a fist slam across his face. He automatically swung into the dark where he sensed the other man was and felt his knuckles connect with a solid mass of flesh.

If Peter felt the blow, he gave no indication. He instantly launched himself at Jason, forcing Williams into the wall.

Grabbing Peter's wrists, Jason struggled to hold him off.

"Damn it, Peter! It's me!" he shouted. "Snap out of it!"

"Die, stupid bitch!" Peter cried out in a voice suddenly so alien. "The Ref-ah-eem are coming!"

With more strength than Jason would have expected, Peter twisted out of his hands and began pummeling his midsection relentlessly. Gasping for breath, Jason finally blocked the onslaught and thrust his fist into Peter's solar plexus.

With rapid-fire blows, Jason forced Peter up the hall, toward the kitchen. He could hear Matt's voice calling his name. Peter snarled like a wild creature, heedless of the blood cascading down his face.

In the dim glow of a distant emergency light, Jason was shocked by what he saw. The body was that of the man who had worked with him over the last two years, but the eyes... There was something in them that could only be described as inhuman.

Then, for an instant, they almost flared with some internal fire.

It was as if Peter were a costume whose true occupant only revealed itself through the eyes.

"Peter!" Jason commanded. "I don't know what the problem is, but we can figure it out."

With a deep growl, Peter's hands snaked out and grabbed a carving knife from a table nearby. He leaped at Jason with an animal snarl.

Jason struggled to bring the knife down, forcing it from Peter's grip, but the young man was surprisingly strong. Jason managed to knock him back into a cart, which skidded across the room, sending metal pots and pans flying.

Ignoring them, Peter shoved the cart viciously aside and headed toward Jason with a deadly gleam in his eyes.

Where are the others? He wondered as he blocked Peter's arm in mid-swing.

Even as the thought came to him, Jason found the grip he needed. He brought Peter's arm down hard against the counter. There was a distinct crack as the bone snapped, but Peter ignored it and twisted in Jason's grasp.

The younger man held the knife high overhead, intent on driving it into Jason.

As the knife came down in a gleaming arc, Jason expertly deflected the deadly blade. With maximum force, he slammed the knife back into Peter's chest.

The young man gasped. For a brief moment, he looked at Jason with shock. Then he collapsed to the floor.

Taking ragged gulps of air, Peter clutched his wound and rolled to one side. Jason immediately descended to the fallen man.

"Call 911!!" he shouted hoarsely as Matt ran into the room. "Peter's been stabbed!"

He yanked a towel from the counter nearby and began working on the wound, trying to staunch the blood.

"I tried…." Carrie sobbed, clutching her phone. "It's dead."

"Call them, damn it!"

Matt rushed to the phone on the counter, but a roar of static left him jerking the headset away from his head in pain.

"Just static!"

"It's too late, anyway." Jason said, slumping with exhaustion. "He's dead."

Carrie screamed, retreating back the way she had come.

Karen entered with a gasp. After a moment, she strode purposefully to the delivery entrance and yanked the door handle violently.

"It's locked."

"Here I have the code," Matt raced over to the door, pulling out what looked like a credit card. He swiped it through the small, black reader by the door handle and punched in a short stream of numbers.

Nothing happened

Trying the sequence once more, he growled in frustration and slammed his fist against the steel door.

"Damn!"

"Well, don't you have regular keys?" Karen cried out.

"No, Donaldson insisted on all this make-you-feel-safe, post-9/11 electronic shit. It's all over the building!"

Karen fruitlessly tried the door again, pulling with both hands on the knob, but it refused to budge. The others began to try the windows with the same results.

Cookie came dashing into the kitchen a look of absolute terror on her face. "We're locked in! I can't open the front doors!"

40

Scott walked briskly up the stairs, herding the reporter ahead of him. The two had progressed as high as the third floor before Skyler finally dug in her heels and wheeled on her cameraman.

"What the hell do you think you are doing?"

"My job, remember!" Scott spat out. "You're the one harping about getting the story, getting the film. Well, here we are!"

He brought the camera up and focused, providing his own angrily extemporaneous narration.

"Tell us, Skyler, when did you first realize you were a world class bitch?"

"You're fired!" She screamed.

"Why, whatever is the matter," he mocked as he moved in closer, keeping the lens trained on her vitriolic response.

Her face contorted in an angry caricature of humanity as she struggled to respond.

What was that?

It seemed that, for a moment, the reporter's face had...*morphed* into something else. Scott became aware of a change in himself as well. This relentless, angry taunting wasn't him at all. Yet, it was as if he was powerless to stop. He lowered the camera in sudden disgust.

"You filthy pig," Skyler growled.

She began forming her next insult when her eyes grew suddenly wide in alarm. Her mouth moving wordlessly, she pointed down the hall behind him.

"What is it?" Scott asked, looking over his shoulder. There was nothing there.

"What the hell is your problem?"

Her only response was a strangled groan as she spun around and dashed off down the darkened hallway.

"There's nothing there!"

Regaining what vestiges of sanity and decency he could muster, Scott found himself suddenly torn between the desire to leave and the knowledge that he should go after her.

She had looked really scared, he thought. *If she wasn't such a pain in the ass....*

He had started down the stairs, fully prepared to leave her behind, when he stopped short. Despite how vile she could be, he couldn't leave the woman alone to face whatever dangers this hotel held.

Scott glanced back toward the darkened hall down which Skyler had raced hysterically. It seemed limitless seconds passed until the angel on his shoulder finally won out.

Reluctantly, he turned to follow her into the darkness.

41

After a fruitless search for an exit, the group returned to the lobby. Shade sat with Yellow Wolf, scrolling through the mysterious knowledge locked away in her NetFone while Matt and Karen worked to bring the lobby's large fireplace to life. A bit of warmth and light, they hoped, would push back some of the darkness that had settled upon them.

Like a doting mother, Cookie Daniels fussed over Carrie, whose injured leg was now propped up on the couch.

"I think it's broken, dear," the older woman said, her brow furrowed with concern. "Should we find Scott? Didn't he say he was once a paramedic or something?"

"It's okay," Carrie piped up weakly. "I can move it some. I think it's just sprained."

"Matt," Cookie begged. "We've got to get out of here!"

With an abrupt roar of frustration, Jason picked up an antique brass floor lamp and slammed it like a baseball bat into the large front windows.

The sudden outburst sent a bolt of fear through the others who flinched collectively.

With a loud whack, he smashed at the large pane a second time. The glass remained intact, although the lamp was a clear causality.

Tossing it aside, Jason peered along the edge of the glass. In one corner, he could just make out the tiny writing:

Kleer Shield
High Impact Polymer
Shatter Proof

"Son of a bitch!" Jason exclaimed as he slammed his fist against the glass. The group jolted. Expressions ranging from wary to worried could be found on each face.

"Why didn't it break?" Cookie asked softly in confusion, standing by Carrie's side.

"This stuff's designed to withstand a terrorist assault," Matt spoke up, hoping the look on his face conveyed the sympathy he felt.

"Matt," Jason exclaimed. "Think! There has to be some way around this security system."

Matt simply shook his head, at a loss for anything to say.

"Jason," a voice spoke up timidly in the strained silence. "I might be able to get us out of here, if I can get some of our equipment working again."

Carrie appeared weak, but Jason could see a fire of determination flickering behind her thick frames. He knew she was smart. She knew electronics. She could do this.

"Do it," Jason said tersely. "I'm going to take care of Peter." He strode like a fuming storm from the room and into the darkness beyond.

With a surge of renewed energy, Carrie struggled to prop herself up. She grabbed her laptop, switched it on, and waited for some assurance that it hadn't been totally fried.

"You really should rest." Cookie warned the girl.

"I'm fine," Carrie replied as she shrugged off the woman's attempt to stop her.

Cookie drew back, dejected.

"But you can help," Carrie added with a smile.

"Sure thing, dear. What can I do?"

"Can you bring me those patch cords and that red bag?"

"You have a plan?" Matt asked as he approached.

"We covered the building in sensors," Carrie explained as she inserted several cords into the ports flanking her laptop.

"How does that help us?" Karen asked, stepping away from the hearth to join the others in the glow around Carrie's laptop.

"There is a backup copy of the program on here. We were using it to test alternate routing systems in order to check air flow. We tied our setup into the security system to remotely verify if any doors or windows were open."

"Thanks for letting me know," Matt said with an exasperated grin.

"No, we didn't damage anything," Carrie protested apologetically. "We just used an empty data port in the system's central node."

"It's okay," Matt chuckled. "That's the least of our problems."

"I'm sorry, dear." Cookie sidled up to the young woman, peering over her shoulder. "I'm still not getting it."

"If we can get enough juice together to send a signal out over the system, I can run a diagnostic for any shorts, and exploit them."

"So, if whatever is locking us in is electrical," Matt asked, "it will have a readable signature we can track?"

"Exactly," Carrie said. "Maybe I can find some way to disengage one of the locks—even if it's just on a window."

"That's great, dear." Cookie said with an edge of concern. "But suppose the window you get open is on the top floor."

"One bridge at a time," Matt suggested. "Carrie, while you're at it, see if you can track down what's powering this lockdown. Maybe we can bypass something. Or just smash it all to hell."

"I'm on it."

"And if it's not electrical," Karen asked.

Carrie looked at the woman blankly. "What else could it be?"

"I mean, what if it's not manmade? Not human? Can you track that as well?"

42

Peter's ruined form lay beneath the white sheet on the kitchen floor, casting a dark shadow in Jason's heart. His prior burst of anger had drained from him as soon as he saw the man's body. He hated what had happened. He hated what he had been forced to do.

Still, no matter how justified or accidental, the fact remained: He had killed Peter.

No sense in dwelling on that now, Jason thought darkly. We might all be dead soon.

He didn't want to admit it, but this hotel was getting to him. He might even have to agree with some of what Shade had been saying, although he was loath to admit it.

But if any part of him had been compromised, forced in to killing Peter, he owed it to the young man to find out. He would take a second look at everything in this building.

He needed to reevaluate the situation, to look at it as if he were still a cop.

For one thing, he would be trying to find out what had triggered Peter's insane personality change. For another, just what was the old man doing down here anyway?

One way to find out, Williams thought.

Half an hour later, balanced on his haunches in the belly of the well, he reluctantly had to shake his head. Nothing.

He had examined every crevice of the place and there was no indication that anything had been staged. The jumble of human bones—itself, a worrisome sight—lay amid fallen stones in bed of oily looking soil.

A low sound brought his head up to listen. It sounded like a generator or a motor in the distance. *Maybe the heat and air system is someplace nearby*, he thought.

He scanned the light across each wall, stopping now and then to run a finger over a stone.

Nothing.

Stooping to examine the rubble closer, Jason now spotted a large flat stone along the wall at the bottom of the well.

Training the flashlight's brilliant beam on its surface, Jason could faintly make out markings. It looked like writing, but in something clearly not English.

Odd, he thought. *What could something like this be doing down here?*

His mind ran through the possibilities: A broken piece of monument, maybe a headstone. Damaged fragments were often sold as rubble. An Indian artifact? Somehow, he didn't think so. He recalled dimly that most tribes lacked a written language.

Curious, he felt for its edges, tugging at each finger hold. As bits of rock and mortar crumbled away, he felt himself gaining a tighter hold on the slab of stone.

Maybe that archaeologist can make sense of it. Jason knew he was grasping at anything that might explain tonight. Ruefully, he admitted that included the irrational.

With a final tug, the stone fell free, bringing with it a large section of wall.

Jason rocked back on his heels as an opening beyond coughed out a shower of dust and debris.

Once the air had settled, Jason wiped his eyes and spotted a black void where the strange stone once lay. Half-forgotten dreams from his childhood slithered unbidden into his mind, glimpses of decaying creatures lurking in wait for the unwary and monsters that lingered within in shadows of fear.

A faint sigh of air, fetid and cloying, crawled from the opening to whisper like splintered glass across his skin. An icy pressure leaned against him—an intimate and ghastly unseen presence, insistent and strong. Jason had the strangest image of some malevolent infant struggling to escape its womb.

He peered deeper into the dark, his heart pounding a ponderous cadence in his chest.

The low hum started again.

Instead of a nebulous noise from some indeterminate corner, it was now an icy grip that reached out from the dark maw.

Jason hunched over in pain, clenching his sides as he shivered uncontrollably.

Run! Hurry!

Jason could not tell where the voice came from, but he knew a good idea when he heard one. His response was automatic and primeval.

Lifting up the large stone with a groan, Jason shoved it up the stone wall and pushed it over the edge. He then leaped onto the ladder and scrambled quickly out of the well.

43

"It's certainly old," Karen acknowledged.

She felt their eyes scrutinizing her as she stood over the mysterious, fractured stone Jason had hauled up from the well. She was trying her best to fathom what she could, but her education was failing her.

"But without studying it back at the lab," she continued, "I can't tell you much more."

"It looks like cuneiform," Shade remarked as she touched the inscribed stone. "Maybe Ugaritic or something older, like Sumerian."

"You can read this?" Karen asked.

"I can try," Shade replied as she pulled out her NetFone. "I think I have some lexicons loaded in here that might help."

"The real mystery remains," Karen wondered aloud. "What was it doing down there?" She bent over the table to scrutinize its surface more closely.

First, the sword and now this stone. What was going on?

From where she stood, Karen could see the weariness creeping into each of their faces. Carrie sat hunched over a small table, her brow frequently knitting in frustration as she worked at restoring the connections to the various sensors. Matt stood to one side; his face inscrutable beneath some dark thought.

Everyone turned as they saw Skyler descending the stairs. She wore a distracted, almost lost expression. Without so much as a glance toward the group gathered around the strange monolith, the reporter moved directly to the bar set up along the check in counter and began mindlessly pouring shot after shot from a tall bottle of some amber liquid.

Moments later, another figure resolved from the shadowy mouth of the grand staircase. Scott, too, looked haggard, as if he had waged some fierce battle on the floor above.

While he nodded wearily to the group, he made no sound as he slid onto a nearby sofa. His eyes closed instantly, and it seemed to Karen, he immediately fell asleep.

What went on up there? She wondered. Karen had no time to ruminate on the animosity between Skyler and her cameraman, a much greater mystery now plagued the guests.

"Got it!" Shade exclaimed, looking up from her database.

"What does it say?" Matt asked.

"Well, the letters are worn and somewhat fragmented." She furrowed her brow as she scrolled through her notes once more. "But it seems to read: *'Ili something 'Abduka 'Ami*.... And I can't quite make out the rest."

"Okay..." Jason drawled. "Mind telling us what that means?"

Karen heard his voice take on a hard edge.

"Patience, oh joyous one. I'm getting there." Shade ran her finger down the touch-screen again, revealing her translation. "It roughly means: 'Hail, Oh...' something I can't make out. 'I am your servant...' and I can't quite read the rest."

"I'm sorry," Jason sighed wearily. "I can't buy this crap."

"I'm glad we have the calm, rational voice of science here," Shade muttered, sotto voce.

"That is not helping," Matt began.

"This whole thing is one huge publicity stunt." Jason pointed angrily to Skyler who could only manage to respond with a blank stare. "I'm not sure how you've done it—yet. But believe me, I will find out before all this is over."

"You're an asshole," Skyler stated flatly, as she began regaining focus. "Why would I screw up my own party?"

"I can't begin to fathom your twisted motivations, but if I find out that you've rigged all this for ratings or something, I will make you pay!"

There was a sudden charge to the environment.

"Hey, guys!" Carrie called out, but her voice was swallowed by the argument at hand.

"I'll sue your slanderous ass into the ground, Williams!" The woman shot back, as she moved in close. "When I'm finished, you won't be able to find a job as a security guard!"

"Guys!" Carrie shouted more urgently.

"Look at Carrie's leg!" Jason yelled, looming over the woman. Skyler had planted herself closer to him. Jason felt his fists curl and a white hot anger boil beneath his self-restraint.

"Peter did that!" The reporter snarled. "He was your man!"

"Wouldn't be the first time some publicity stunt went wrong."

"Publicity stunt, my ass!"

Shade caught the look on Carrie's face.

"We have to get out of here, now!" Carrie yelled, frantically pointing to the screens in front of her. "Jason! Jason! It's back!"

A rumbling caught everyone's attention as the floor vibrated. Scott opened his eyes wide in alarm. Everyone jumped to their feet. Furniture moved by itself and Cookie clutched at Matt. Karen grabbed the table with the stone while Shade scowled at the two people still snarling like rabid dogs, oblivious to what was happening.

Shade felt it. Something wrapped itself around those two, twisted between them, and dug itself into their minds—their souls.

"Nobody's going anywhere!" Skyler screamed out. "I have signed contracts from each of you!"

"You can't hold us to that now!" Cookie screeched as she clutched Matt tighter.

To Shade it seemed as if a fog of hate had slowly built up in the room

"Hey, psycho Barbie!" Shade shouted. "Back off!"

Like exhausted boxers, Jason and Skyler fell back to their respective corners. Jason shook himself like a dog emerging from a lake. Skyler marched across the room to her half-abandoned bottle of Scotch and poured shot after shot until she slumped into an overstuffed chair.

Shade could see the rancor slip from the room like a serpent to retreat back toward the kitchen, toward the well.

44

After the dust settled, Karen turned back to the stone. Pulling a sable brush from her carryall, she began dusting away bits of plaster that had rained down from the ceiling. As she worked, the cuneiform letter came into sharper relief, better revealing the inscription.

How did something like this end up in Corvus Mound, of all places?

She glanced at the carryall and the impossible sword hidden within. Her mind drifted on various hypotheses, each less probable than the last. With an embarrassed chuckle, she dismissed them all as foolish romanticism and returned to the others.

"What if we are approaching this wrong?" Karen said, drawing everyone's attention. "In 1957, a stone was found not far from here incised with letters of the Runic alphabet—the language of the several Germanic peoples, including the Norse."

"You mean like Vikings?" Matt wore a look of deep confusion. "They weren't here in Oklahoma."

"Exactly," Karen replied. "It was for that very reason that many dismissed the stone as a hoax. Most refused to believe it could be real because we had history all laid out."

"Is there a point to all of this?" Jason barked.

Ignoring him, Karen continued. "Let's assume we don't know as much as we think about the past. What if we've been missing the truth by ignoring the anomalies?"

"What anomalies?"

"Like this inscription. Like the swor—" Karen stopped herself. *Better to not mention that yet.* "Most who studied the stone agreed that it read: 'This land belongs to Medok. This land is his'."

"Jesus!" Jason interjected. "And to think *you* were the horse I was betting on!"

"Medok?" Shade suddenly sat up, alert. "Did you say Medok? Why didn't you say something earlier?"

"Why, what do you know?" Karen turned to look at Shade who was busy scrolling through the digital depths of her electronic device.

"I'm not sure yet, but I think Medok is...." The young woman's voice trailed off as she became engrossed in some unfathomable thought.

"Well," Karen said. "If you've got a minute, I've uncovered some of the missing letters on the stone."

At this, Shade's concentration was shattered. She look up at Karen.

"Show me!"

45

Outside the hotel, the night air nearly burst with humidity. The scent of ozone and fresh soil hung over a deserted main street, heralding the arrival of the thunderstorms that had been erupting throughout the county all evening.

A flurry of trash skidded down the street, momentarily taking flight, before becoming ensnared in the branches of a nearby tree.

Bursts of brilliant white blossomed within the roiling sky as internal lightning flared. With each flash, the storm crept closer, as if a predator stalking the small town.

A deep rumble of thunder shook the air, sending percussive waves out to rattle windows throughout town.

A small storefront sidled up next to the Montford Arms, as if to hug it for protection. Flickering from behind its large picture window, an array of televisions broadcast various programs.

Almost lost among the toothpaste ads and insipid comedies, Everett Reed, Channel 6's meteorologist, gesticulated wildly against the multicolored radar image. Tornado warnings peppered the map, forming along a large crescent-shaped dry line that hung over eastern Oklahoma like a scythe. Several enhanced F-5 twisters had already touched down with devastating results.

Channel 6, in its usual tabloid fashion, had worked the graphics department hard to craft the most sensational title card they could muster on such short notice: *Funnels of Fury!*

Beneath him, on a ticker, scrolled the names of those towns at highest risk: Bokoshe, Pocola, Braden, Corvus Mound....

Overhead, swirling into life like some Lovecraftian beast, a massive thunderhead churned angrily.

46

Shade and Karen stood perched over the ancient tablet, working with the archaeologist's many brushes and tools, in an effort to clean up the emerging text.

As the burning welts return, Shade spotted the other woman rubbing her hand absently.

"I saw you rubbing your hand earlier...."

"Yeah," Karen said, looking down to find her own welts had re-emerged. "I think it's an allergic reaction to something, maybe in the lab."

"I'm not so sure," Shade intoned significantly as she showed the woman her own. "Have you had the dreams?"

Karen shot the young woman a startled glance. "How did you...."

"The beast?"

"Yes...."

It was now clear to Shade. By some unknown design, they had both been drawn to this place, at this time. There could be no mistake; Karen was the woman the warrior had asked her to help.

"We've got it!" Shade exclaimed.

The others gathered around the table where the two women had been working.

"You've translated it?" Matt asked as he pushed his way through to the stone.

"Yes, with Karen's help."

She had read so much about the culture, it should have been obvious. The clues were there the whole time in paintings, on countless carvings, and now incised into the face of this mysterious tablet.

"So...." Jason begged impatiently. "What does it say?"

Calling up the note on her NetFone, Shade cleared her throat and began reading another nonsensical string of gutturals.

"Ili Moti! 'Abduka 'Ami Wa-du 'Olamika."

"Still sounds like Klingon," Scott joked weakly.

"Karen and I have translated this as: 'Hail! Oh, Mot. I am your servant and your eternal slave'."

"So, who's Mot?" Matt asked, voicing the question on everyone's mind.

"Mot," Shade explained, "is an ancient Mesopotamian death god."

"Who," Karen added importantly, "also went by the name Meldoch or Medok."

"Unfortunately, we haven't yet figured out exactly who he was."

"Or," Karen added, "why we would find his name carved in stone halfway around the world?

A sudden chime alerted Shade that her database has finished its search through terabytes of digitized documents. An answer awaited her.

"Found another reference," she said, turning to Karen. "It mentions the slayers of Mot and their consecrated swords."

At the mention of swords, Karen visibly started.

"My bag!"

All eyes watched as she hastily retrieved her carryall from the table. To their astonishment, she reached in and withdrew a short-bladed sword. Holding it up, she looked around the group.

"The other day I was digging at the Mounds, when I unearthed this."

"Wow!" Carrie said, as she eyed the object.

Aged as it was, the lethal power of the sword was clear. No show piece, but a working weapon for a warrior.

"I was afraid of site contamination," Karen shared. "But after what Shade just said…."

"Can I see that," Shade asked.

Matt frowned as he saw the sword.

"You say you found that in one of the mounds?" he asked.

"What is it?" Shade questioned.

"I have one just like that back in the office."

"Let me see." Karen told him.

Following Matt down the corridor, the group crowded into his office.

"I've been staring at it for months," he told them, as he pulled it down from the wall. "I even thought about swiping it."

"How long has it been here?" Karen asked, as she took in the spiraling pattern on the hilt. In nearly every way, it was identical to the one she held. "It must have been contamination, after all. Someone brought the mate out to the mounds and buried it."

"No, I don't think that's the case." Matt spoke uncomfortably. "I know this will sound… crazy. At least, it did to me."

"What?" Karen urged.

"It's all coming together," Shade announced. "I think I am beginning to understand what we may be dealing with."

A soft laughter erupted from the doorway. Everyone turned in unison to find Matt's grandfather standing there, shaking his head.

"Young lady," Ben chuckled. "You don't know the half of it."

47

"Okay, Ben. Help us," Karen demanded. "What's going on here?"

The group had all ranged themselves around Matt's grandfather who sat deep within the supple contours of the large leather chair at Matt's desk.

"For most of my life I have skated by, thinking that I wouldn't have to face this. Too long I thought that *you* would never have to face it either, Matt." A pained expression clouded the old man's face. "I was wrong. I was arrogant, and probably more than a little stupid. Fate doesn't pass us by because we ignore it. I can tell you a lot of things. The question is will you believe the unbelievable?"

"The unbelievable?" Shade rejoined. "That's any given Tuesday for me."

Jason frowned at her, and then turned back to the old man, "Why don't you give us a chance to find out?"

"Our family has been the guardians of a secret almost as old as time itself. We are the *Khaldis*.

Many millennia ago, my ancestors carried an ancient evil from their homeland in order to save our people.

The stories tell us we traveled for years over harsh desert, across rugged mountains, and through vast wastelands. We crossed the mighty waters to this world. The journey was cruel and long and many people died along the way."

"Finally, we found a place—this place—and we buried the evil. Perhaps we should not have tried to move it. "

Ben sat still for so long; Matt grew concerned, edging closer, his brows furrowed.

"Grandpa?" he asked with concern.

"Got to get it said, Matt. After all these years...."

Ben ran a hand through his hair, wincing as he encountered a tender spot. "Life in this new world was unexpectedly harsh. So many died before they could pass on their knowledge, their wisdom.

As the guardians, we knew the rituals—or so we thought. We had lived here only a few years before the evil began to crawl slowly from its grave. It seeped into the people's hearts and turned them against one another.

That was when we learned how little we really knew. We couldn't fully contain the evil as the old ones had. What we did was only a bandage. The rituals had to be repeated regularly to keep it contained.

In time, others arrived and we stayed hidden for a while."

"You mean the Europeans?" Jason asked.

"He means Native Americans," Karen injected without taking her eyes from Ben.

"Native Americans?" Scott wore a confused expression. "Isn't *he* Native American?"

"Ben's story," Karen added with a look of vindication, "goes back much, much further than that. Maybe as much as 50,000 years."

"Is that possible?" Jason questioned. "That's not what I remember from history."

"There's a lot that didn't make it into the history books," Karen countered.

"Deal with the questions later, okay?" Matt suggested. "Let's hear what Ben has to say."

"Our numbers were small by then. We aligned ourselves with these people, always keeping our duty clear in our minds," Ben said. "We continued to stand guard through all the years. We would continue to be the Khaldis, the priests of the Creator and servants to *She Who Walks Between Worlds*. But without the sacred knowledge…. Well, there was only so much the priests could do. Every so often the evil would seep out."

No one moved and the only sound was the old man's words. Time itself seemed to pause with portent.

"The hotel had only been open about five years when a guest began to visit. Maybe once a year at first and then, later, he seemed to live here. He appeared wealthy and charming on the surface. That was how he was able to smooth talk his way into a circle of wealthy and bored men. He was always spouting some nonsense about a new world order. He seemed to have an uncanny ability to zero in on the weakest part of anyone."

Ben adjusted himself in the chair as he collected his thoughts. "With this man's arrival…. Well, evil had always been around here, but it really stirred when this man arrived. I believe that the evil my people buried so long ago reaches out and tries to gain control. With some, it finds a seed of anger or fear and helps it grow into an ugly, dangerous weed."

"Like all those fights we've been having," Matt noted.

"Yes," Ben agreed. "Unfortunately, with others…. Well, say a man was already a bit twisted inside; he might become something worse—much worse.

"Peter!" Carrie breathed.

"He seduced some local men into joining a…." Ben wrestled with the words before tossing them aside with an angry flick of his wrist. "Men's club, my ass! I guess you'd call it a cult. They called themselves the *Followers of Rephaim*."

Shade, at hearing this, dove once more into her electronic library.

"They thought it was great fun at first."

"Drunken rituals in the dead of night?" Jason asked.

"Yes," Ben nodded. "After awhile, all that changed. Every perversion known was made a part of their ceremonies."

Thunder exploded outside as the promised storm intensified. Fierce winds buffeted the building.
Shade ignored it all, concentrating on her search. Something was echoing somewhere deep within her. Like a maniacal shell game, she tried to follow

the missing piece, but at the moment there was only a mounting headache.

"So the fights, the accidents, the deaths?" Matt asked. "They are all a part of this thing trying to get free?"

"Yes, Matt." Ben dipped his head, shaking it slightly. "I feel like I have let you down."

"I don't disagree that *something* is going on," Jason interjected. "In fact, I'm pretty convinced of that. I just can't buy this ancient evil crap."

"It's a better explanation," Shade pointed out, "than some nefarious scheme cooked up by that Mensa candidate you've been blaming."

"Jason," Carrie added. "You saw Peter, how different he was. That monster was not the man we knew."

"Carrie," Jason replied patiently. "Peter was brilliant, no doubt. But he was also troubled in many ways, which is why we don't need to grasp at supernatural explanations for what happened."

"Maybe you're right." Carrie conceded. "But, Jason, what if there *is* something else going on here?"

"Look," Scott broke in. "I'm no scientist or shaman or whatever. But I know we're trapped in here with some weird shit going down. I don't much care about the whys. I just want to get out of here."

"Our sensors," Jason admitted, "recorded some anomalies when the event occurred. Somewhere in that data, Carrie hopes to find a weakness in the system that will get us all out of here."

"Excellent idea," Shade offered, much to the man's surprise. "While they work on the locks, the rest of us will explore other...alternatives."

Imperceptibly, the young goth had taken charge, doling out tasks to each of them.

Shade turned to face Karen. "You and me are going to find out more about this stone."

"Let's do it," Karen agreed.

"Good. Ben, if you can, tell Matt every last thing you know and more about your rituals. We need every bit of help we can get."

Yellow Wolf nodded curtly, his face taking on a grave and stately expression.

"Scott," Shade continued. "If you would do me a favor...."

"Anything, babe," he assured with a wink.

"Can you keep Skyler out of our hair?"

"Can I tranquilize her?" he asked with a hopeful expression.

"Maybe you should just tie her up."

With a click of his heels, Scott stood erect and waved her a brisk salute. "Aye, aye!"

Shade smiled and then turned to Cookie.

"I've got a big job for you."

"Yes?"

"How good are you at warming up leftovers? I'm starving!"

She would never admit it, Shade knew, but Cookie was grateful to have been given such a mundane task, far from the dangers the others would soon face.

It felt natural giving those orders, as if she had done it a thousand times before. Images of the confident warrior from her dreams sprang to mind, causing her to wonder if this new streak of assertiveness was even her own.

"Well, I guess every battle needs a leader," Matt said, as he helped Ben up. "I'd say we found ours."

Shade only hoped she was up to the challenge.

47

Shade heard a frustrated groan and turned to see Carrie bang her keyboard angrily. The young scientist had been working hard to find a way into the security grid without much success. It was taking a noticeable toll on the otherwise reserved woman.

"What's the problem?" Shade asked, crossing over to the nest of electronic gear in the lobby's far corner.

"Oh, it's this subroutine!" Carrie heaved exhaustedly. "I can't get it to work right. If Peter were—"

Shade saw the girl wince as the painful memory blossomed in her mind.

"I'm no whiz like my partner," Shade offered, "But I do know a thing or two about programming."

"Your partner?"

"My business partner, Kevin, and I own a software company: Byte Marks."

"Zombie Cheerleaders?" For a moment, Carrie seemed to forget her anguish. "That's you?"

"You've played it?" Shade was surprised.

"It's one of my favorites," she exclaimed brightly. "I especially like how when you decapitate them, their heads deflate and shoot off like a balloon."

"Well, I figured that's what happens to air heads," Shade informed her with a devious grin.

Another strident chirrup from Carrie's computer sent her elated spirits crashing once more

"Ugh! There it goes again."

"Well, let's see what we can figure out."

Shade pulled up another chair. Her fingers danced over the keys swiftly, as her eyes remained fixed on lines of dense code.

Within minutes, Shade and Carrie had hacked their way deep into the complex web of commands, seeking out the countless barricades that prevented them from interfacing with the security system.

"You know, I've been thinking," Carrie said as the two waited for another download to finish. "Physicists have toyed with the idea that there isn't just one universe, but maybe a whole string of them."

"The Multiverse," Shade acknowledged.

"Exactly. Each universe connects to the others into infinity." Peter believed this could explain many paranormal phenomena."

"What was his idea?"

"He believed the density in the barriers separating universes wasn't entirely uniform," Carried explained, recalling just how bright and intelligent Peter had actually been. "In some places, they could wear thin, giving us a glimpse at another time or place."

"Or allow something to cross over," Shade mused darkly. "Either way, to us, it would seem like a ghost."

"Yes," Carrie agreed. "When it was only a thinning in the fabric of the universe."

A new error message drew another complaint from the Carrie.

"I thought that might happen. Try this." Shade said, tapping in a string of code.

"Awesome!" Carrie called out as she typed in several more lines. "I didn't even think of that. Thanks, that makes a lot more sense."

"Anytime," Shade said as she pulled out her NetFone. "Damn."

"What's wrong," Carrie asked without looking up from her screen.

"Battery's about to die on this thing. Mind if I plug it into your generator?"

"Of course," Carrie assured her with a smile. "That thing seems to be coming in handy."

"Let's hope," Shade replied with a shrug. She was warming up to the young scientist, who seemed to grow more confident even as so many others were succumbing to the evil that permeated the hotel. "Okay, I'm going to run up and get my charger."

"Is that safe?" Carrie asked with a slight frown.

"We'll see," Shade said with a sigh, as she snatched a flashlight from the table and ascended the stairs into the darkness above.

When she arrived at the landing, she moved forward cautiously, steeling herself for whatever might be lurking in the dark recesses along the dim corridor. There were even fewer emergency lights here: one at the landing and another in the distance, at the far end of the hall.

Shade had been through her share of haunted houses and encountered more than a few dark entities, but nothing on the scale she had witnessed at the Montford Arms. It had her on edge and she didn't like it.

She proceeded to her room, thankful no monsters had leapt at her from the shadows. In fact, only the muffled howl of wind and the peal of thunder managed to penetrate the stillness.

She slipped the old key into the lock, and slid inside quickly.

Grabbing the charger, she glanced around; searching for anything else that might prove useful. After a moment scrutinizing the contents of her pack, she snatched a handful of spare batteries and a small case.

Inside this was an array of herbs, both medicinal and magical, as well as several ampoules filled with mysterious concoctions. These were a gift from the eccentric Wiccan whom she had come to think of as her mother for the past eight years.

A sudden sound drew her eyes back to the open doorway behind her, but nothing stirred. However, she could sense a malignant presence slinking about furtively.

She stuffed the items into the pockets of her long coat and stepped into the hall.

The air around her became charged with a sudden burst of electricity, and she grew dizzy. Her hand stung once more as the familiar red welts returned.

"Ow!" She cried. The episodes were getting worse.

Images from the dream returned unbidden to her mind. She saw the woman again. She was speaking, but Shade couldn't hear the words. Something, like the roar of a waterfall, drowned them out.

Shade felt a shiver course up her back, and she spun to see a figure closing in on her from the shadows that crouched just beyond the reach of her flashlight.

She spotted the glint of something gold swinging pendulously against the silhouette as it neared.

Within moments, the figure resolved to reveal a man dressed in tattered, blood-stained rags of some bygone era. His mutilated face was a mask of vacant eyes and a gaping black orifice. His two bony claws reached out for her as a foul odor filled the corridor. A wave of terror, cold as an arctic blast, surged toward Shade. She shivered heavily, but did not move as she felt something happen.

Like sinking into a warm bath, Shade felt herself suffused in some strange energy. Her hand rose without command and she heard herself, as if from a distance, speak in an alien tongue.

"TAH! Yit besh birkin sahm 'El gezir!"

A rumble, louder than thunder, rolled through the hallway as the creature was swept away in a flash.

Just as quickly, the iciness dissipated, leaving Shade stunned and alone in the empty hall.

"What the hell was that?"

48

"We are being trapped and hunted by a demon from the ancient Middle East" Shade announced matter-of-factly as they gathered to hear what more she and Karen had learned.

"Ben's crazy tale aside, what would that have to do with us?" Jason asked.

"The Sumerians and others," Shade continued, "had a pantheon of deities that included Mot—or Medok—one bad dude who rampaged throughout the land, killing thousands. His minions, the Repha'im, in the guise of crows or flies, would then carry the newly-harvested souls off to the underworld."

"We need to be running the data and not listening to fairy tales!" Jason began, but Matt held up to silence him.

"I take it you are basing this on something?" Matt asked.

"Yes," Shade assured him. "It's all there: the crows, The Followers of Repha'im, Ben's story and... Anath."

"What's Anath?" Cookie asked.

"In many ways, that was the key." Shade explained. "Ben told us the Khaldis were servants to 'she who walks between worlds,' which struck me as oddly poetic. I looked it up."

"And?" Jason looked at her expectantly.

"The phrase applies to another figure in the same pantheon: Anath. She was a warrior and the daughter of 'El, the supreme deity."

"So, how does she figure in," Matt asked.

"She and her sister, Asherah, hunted Mot, who had taken the form of a terrible hulking beast." She nodded to Ben. "Once weakened by the women's swords, the Khaldis were then able to perform the ritual that cast Mot into the depths of hell."

"So, let me get this straight." Jason folded his arms as he donned an incredulous expression. "Some ancient demon was buried here by Matt's ancestors and now it's waking up and trying to kill us?"

"Good," Shade said flatly. "You've been paying attention."

"There is a line of thinking," Karen interjected, "that all mythology has a basis in fact."

"I need more than that," Jason exclaimed.

"This place has always been strange," Karen offered. "Full of anomalies we archaeologists dismissed as contamination from pranksters or pot hunters. During my own dig, I was finding symbols that bore striking resemblance to those excavated in ancient Iraq."

"So, my grandfather is right," Matt admitted. "It's all true."

"More than that," said Shade as she raised her eyes from the device in her hand to look him in the eye. "We know how to stop it."

49

"Are we all clear now on what to do?" Shade asked the group gathered around the largest of the dining room tables.

"Not clear at all," Jason tossed in as he glanced at the rest of the group. "But I know what *I'm* going to do."

Shade glanced through the entrance into the lobby where Skyler sat, still fuming in the chair where Scott had tied her.

Cookie assisted Carrie who worked furiously at her equipment. The two women looked like they could gladly give some serious damage to the newswoman given half a chance.

Shade was relieved everyone would be contained in one area. If they pulled this off, it would be good to get out of here all at once—and quickly.

On the table was an assortment of objects that Ben said would be necessary for the ritual as well as a notepad containing observations on all that Shade could learn about the entity.

In pride of place were the small bronze flask, which served as a talisman for the ritual, and the spiral-incised swords.

The beauty of the plan is its simplicity, Shade thought as they left the others and made their way toward the lower levels. A straight-ahead attack, at least she hoped that would be the case.

Once more, she reviewed the steps in her head: She would use the sword of Anath, Karen would use the sword of Asherah, and Matt would use the flask to conduct the binding ritual.

She hefted the sword in her hands and was again daunted by its weight. Could she do this? She tried to push the doubt from her mind. She had to do it. There was simply no other way.

Piecing together what little they knew, and the insight Shade had cobbled together from the dreams, it had become clear that the entire ritual required more than just the banishing element Matt's ancestors had been performing for millennia. Even lacking one element weakened the entire process, which explained why Ben and those before him had to perform it periodically.

Once the evil manifested itself, it would have been up to Anath and her sister Asherah to attack its physical form, wounding it to such a degree that its grip on this world weakened. This would have given the priests leverage enough to banish the beast from their realm through their ritual.

Yellow-Wolf had been amazed at how much had been lost over the centuries. Shade had been concerned how little they might still know and what that might mean.

Tapping on the screen of her NetFone, Shade began digging into the dark knowledge she had built into her digital grimoire. Somewhere in there she hoped would be the missing pieces to Ben's puzzle. She was all too aware of the strange circumstances woven together to fashion this moment.

This had to be the ultimate example of synchronicity, Shade thought. *Or maybe something larger than us is steering the course?*

50

The night screamed. A powerful wind pounded at the lobby windows as electricity sliced open the dark sky. Scott flinched at the onslaught.

"One…two…" Before he could count to three, thunder racked the building once more. "Damn, it's getting worse!"

"This is gonna be bad, for sure," Ben lamented to no one in particular. He'd experienced too many storms in his life not to recognize the signs.

"Fuck you, old man!" Skyler spat out. Her face was so contorted she was barely recognizable. "The meteorologist at the station said this shit was going to miss us by miles."

Ben didn't bother to react. The evil of the place had dug its claws into the newscaster. He knew her vitriol was a symptom of the monster that infected this hotel, an evil coursing through each of them.

She had been like this since she and the bald man had returned from filming. Those weakest would exhibit symptoms first, he knew. Then the humming would come. Then the deaths.

Matt's steps slowed as he guided them, crawling at times, through the narrow tunnel that led from the large hole created when the carved tablet was removed from the wall of the old well. It descended steeply into the earth below the hotel. The floor beneath them was paved in slabs of stone, forming steps whenever the tunnel made a sudden descent.

The beam of Matt's flashlight quivered and he knocked it impatiently against his leg. This was no time to lose their light.

"It's not the flashlight," Shade whispered softly. She pointed with her head, "Look."

The air ahead glowed faintly. A sickly phosphorescence rendered their own light needless and Matt clicked it off.

Karen suddenly stopped and wrinkled her nose. "What's that smell?!"

Only then did the other two become aware of it.

"It's hell, kids." Shade stated flatly. "What did you expect?" Her mind suddenly recalled the green fog shrouding the Flat Irons and the portent it seemed to have held.

I guess this is it, she thought.

The trio trudged further down to find themselves engulfed in a foul smelling pool of swirling incandescent fog.

"Ugh!" Matt coughed as he covered his nose.

"You didn't think evil smelled nice did you?" Shade called back, her voice muffled by the shirt covering her face.

They kept on until the tunnel widened, suddenly revealing a large chamber. They turned to see a wall of fog crouch in the hallway behind them, as if cutting them off from escape.

As Karen's eyes adjusted, she examined the strange stonework surrounding them. She examined the many symbols scrawled across the walls. Walking through the foul fog, she forced herself to ignore its greedy, greasy embrace.

"The last time I saw symbols like these was in the British Museum," she exclaimed with awe. "They were on an ancient Hittite urn. My God, what is this place?"

"What are these?" Matt peered intently into the gloom overhead where still more strange markings had been carved overhead. "Egyptian?"

"I just can't believe it," Karen exclaimed in hushed, almost reverent tones, but then remained silent for many moments. She was intently examining every square inch.

"What is it?" Matt asked. Still, the archaeologist remained lost in thought. He turned to Shade, searching her face for answers. He was amazed at how quickly he was learning to rely upon her and her gift—and how easily he found himself accepting it all.

Shade simply shook her head.

Finally, Karen spoke softly. "As I excavated the mounds by the river, I had been struck time after time by clues and vague impressions that a larger ceremonial mound existed. I could never find it, but it seemed to be associated with a death cult. I eventually began to assume that the mound had either been razed or cannibalized to build other earthworks...." Karen trailed off and stood, staring at the passage walls.

"What, Karen?" Shade urged.

"This is the mound."

"You mean...."

"Yes, not just a mound but *the* mound. The mother of all mounds." Karen could see her excitement reflected in Shade's eyes. "That 'hill' downtown Corvus sits on *is* that lost mound. It has to be the largest mound in North America!"

With new eyes, the trio examined their surroundings. The gloom was revealing oddly shaped stones, faint columns, and images everywhere.

"They're not just pictorial," Karen informed. "They're spells."

"More spirals over here, Karen!" Shade called from where a faint series of lines traced their way in sinuous intricacy around one of the four pillars.

"The spiral must be part of the ritual." Karen suggested.

"Symbolizing the descent into hell?" Shade asked.

It seemed their insights had come, not merely from their own knowledge, but from something outside themselves.

While Karen and Shade attempted to unravel the mystery surrounding them, Matt watched as a change came over the two women. It was nothing he could articulate, but it was there nonetheless.

"That's great," Matt interjected impatiently shaking off the anxiety he was feeling. "But we have to stop this thing. Come on!"

Matt retrieved the vessel from the bag slung over his shoulder, and knelt—with some degree of hesitancy—into the foul miasma. Carefully, he poured the strange viscous concoction onto the dirt around him.

"Ishk Medoch sunum persh," he called out tentatively, the words echoing absurdly loud within the chamber. He felt completely foolish chanting what to him were only meaningless syllables.

I hope I am saying this right.

Swords at the ready, the two women flanked him. Within moments of beginning the incantation, the words began to have a startling effect.

Swirling eddies of fog began to shrink back from the trio. The movement of the mist seemed almost sentient.

But then it probably was, Matt realized. This thought sent a chill through his core, but he forced himself to continue the chanting.

"Hilka! Hilka!" He took a deep breath. "Hilka!"

Suddenly, the earth shuddered beneath them as shadows began dancing frenetically at their periphery. The glowing fog had now coalesced near a flat, black stone, which held the remains of something once living.

As Matt chanted, it began to shape itself a form that could only vaguely be described as human. I resolved into an anthropomorphic nightmare that grew larger with each passing moment.

Karen screamed involuntarily as a vaporous appendage lashed at the walls around them. The shadows leaped to life and began filling the cavern like a flock of crows—shadowy, wraith-like crows.

As they swept past each of the warriors, the bird-forms slashed at their clothing and tore their skin.

"Aaah! Damn you!" Shade cried out, as she swiped at the creatures with her sword. It had no effect.

Shade glanced over to Karen who was in the same predicament. Out of the corner of her eye, she vaguely registered with some admiration that Matt, battered and bleeding, kept chanting as shadows attacked. Each pass left raw, jagged pain in their wake.

"HILKA! HILKA!" Matt cried with a relentless fervor born of anger and determination.

Even upon entering the chamber, he still harbored doubts as to how real this all was. But now, with an ancient demon waging war upon them…

"TAH!" he growled, commanding the wraiths to leave. In response, a shadow sliced his face and warm blood traced its way toward his mouth.

He spat out a sanguineous glob of saliva and shouted, "Come on mother fuckers! Come on!"

Karen sliced harmlessly through another crow wraith. "Guys! This isn't working!"

Shade was thinking the same thing. "Matt, keep chanting. Karen…Plan B!"

51

The clock on the mantel told the hour.

It was time.

Jason and Carrie worked quickly to finish the job. If they were lucky, they would come out of this with some valuable data as well.

"You've got to check out these readings!" Carrie called out. "It's everything Peter said it would be."

Jason turned to see a phonebook of data scroll across a nearby monitor. The cameras, EVP, and a host of other devices continued to record.

"We can't lose this data, for Pete's sake..." He paused at his unintentional pun. A pang of loss clutched his chest and he heaved a ragged breath.

"I'll start downloading all this while you finish up with the security hack."

"Not long now," she assured him.

Jason knew this was a once-in-a-lifetime opportunity. Amateur ghost hunters tripped over their feet and bumped heads abandoned hospitals for decades and never received a thousandth the data displayed on his equipment now.

52

Karen and Shade, swords in hand, stood back to back in the center of the chamber, near Matt.

"Are you sure this will work?" Karen asked, fear filling her voice.

"It has to." Shade spoke with a confidence she hoped her research warranted. Plan A had been for Matt to conduct Ben's ritual while Karen and Shade wielded the swords at whatever came at them.

Clearly, that's not working, Shade thought.

In a scanned copy of an ancient Akkadian tablet, however, she had found mention of a ritual involving two sacred swords. She only hoped it contained the missing pieces to Ben's ritual.

If this ritual was as powerful as she thought, it went a long way to explaining why someone may have tried to hide one of the swords.

The women placed the tips of their swords into the earth and turned in a clockwise fashion, creating a spiral around them. Once the circle of protection was complete, Shade dug into her jacket and removed her bundle of magical herbs. She selected a particular blend, throwing its contents into the air and letting it waft back onto her and Karen.

She called out, "Ashkim, mehr Anath! Yit besh birkin sahm 'El gezir!"

The effect was instantaneous.

A bolt of light shot up between the two women, illuminating their swords and, more subtly, changing them inside.

Shade was familiar with having another's thoughts in her head, so she wasn't totally unprepared. Still, taking on the presence of Anath, was like downing a fifth of Jack. The impact was more powerful than she had expected.

She could sense Karen's thoughts and emotions, however, and knew they were in turmoil. The young archaeologist was struggling to accept into her being this spirit, this other called Asherah.

In her head, Shade now heard the unfamiliar voices as they spoke to each other.

This one wears armor to protect herself, chuckled the first.

If she is like you, she will soon know her own strength, the other confirmed.

Come, my sister, chided the first. *We did not become 'they who walk between the worlds' to chatter idly like old women. We—and these new warriors—have work to do.*

Focusing, Shade charged ahead, holding the sword before her like a Goth Moses parting the vile, glowing smoke that was encircling them. Matt raced to catch up.

"Whatever you're doing, Shade," Matt shouted, dodging the talons of the dark wraiths. He grimaced as yet another one sliced into his skin, damn! "Don't stop! It's working. These things really don't seem to like that sword now."

53

"Can you do anything with this?" Jason barked minutes later as he struggled to run two units at the same time. Even when the computers had run tests and diagnostics, Jason had never seen this much data flow across their screens.

"I think...." Carrie frowned at the screen, her fingers flying over the keyboard. "Maybe if I try bypassing...."

A small explosion erupted in front of the building and Cookie screamed. The storm focused all of its fury on the hotel, screeching and pounding at the doors as it sought entrance.

Debris whipped wildly outside: a trash can skidded down the street, slamming forcefully into a nearby car. A sign painted with a clown face—

from God knows where—slapped against the window; its grin shone sinister in the bizarre and startling juxtaposition.

The storm was a snarling, spitting, ravenous beast and they were reduced to the roles of sniveling cave dwellers.

"Hurry!" Jason cried out over an ominous roar like a freight train at full speed.

Then the lights went out.

54

Karen's sword grew warm in her hands as she wrapped her fingers tightly around it, drawing its power into her.

Her mind felt crowded with new thoughts and images, which overlapped the present like a waking dream. She was running through the night. The stars overhead were brighter than she had ever seen. The woman was at her side again.

Hurry! Hurry!

Karen shook her head, attempting to dislodge the vision and return her focus to the present. She couldn't afford visions and dreams.

Not now.

She looked at her hand. The scratches were back.

Karen followed Shade into the glowing, green vapor, slashing at the crow wraiths. Fast and relentless, the multitude of wraiths attacked. The newfound power she felt was keeping pace, but these demons were getting their licks in too.

One particularly large and nasty shadow screeched and shot itself toward her. Its impact hit her squarely in the chest, plunging Karen back into the oily fog.

Panicking for a moment as the green cloud hungrily coalesced around her, Karen coughed. She tried to get back up, but lost her balance and fell heavily toward the vapor.

Inside her head, she heard the voice of Asherah. Another surge of the woman's strength flowed through her limbs and Karen launched herself up from the dirt.

Outside her head, she became aware of a strange tattoo—no, a humming. It filled the earthen cavity, saturated the air, and penetrated their bones. Karen could even feel it in her teeth. In seconds, the humming roared and darted around them

Get up! It has begun.

"Ashkim, mehr Anath!" Karen-Asherah chanted. "Yit besh birkin sahm 'El gezir!"

The dark shadows continued swirling high overhead. One slashed at her and she felt a stinging in her arm. Looking down, she spotted a trickle of blood from a small jagged cut.

Enraged, Karen sliced Asherah's sword into a thick convergence of shadows.

With a scream, the dark mass withered away into the mist. Looking around, Karen saw that, although Shade was struggling, her hair matted with sweat and blood, she seemed to be holding her own for the moment.

What about Matt? Where was Matt?

She panicked briefly and then saw his motionless form slumped over in the mist.

"Shade!" She cried. "Matt's hurt!"

An unbearable shriek rang out and the circling shadows transformed once more into the crow wraiths, the Repha'im, who swooped above their heads, their cries blending with the ruthless hum.

"Hurry, Shade! They just keep coming!"

55

"No! No!" Jason cried as the monitors flickered briefly. "Tell me we didn't lose it all."

"We're safe." Carrie told him, not taking her eyes from the screen. "We have redundancies built into the backups."

"Bless you, Carrie." He planted a kiss atop the woman's head. "You are a life saver."

"Not yet," she replied. "But I might be as soon as I...." Typing in the final keystrokes with a flourish, Carrie held up her hands. "It's done."

Jason ran over to the control panel near the main doors and entered the code Matt had given him. With a whoosh, he heard the lock disengage.

Jason's face broke into a large grin, the first in a long while

"Yes!" he yelled.

The wind screamed outside and he could see little but a solid curtain of gun metal rain. Fat marbles of ice impacted the vehicles and buildings lining the street outside. In a sudden burst of lightning, Jason spotted a horrible monster poised to strike. Clinging to the bottom of the dark, bilious wall was a fat rope of destruction. Already he could see it chewing its way through the far edge of town, kicking up debris like confetti.

Another flash of lightning briefly illuminated a bright yellow sign.

"Scott!" he shouted. "There's an old movie theater across the street. It has a fallout shelter. We need to get everybody over there now!"

"Why can't we just stay here?" Skyler demanded. As if in response, a shudder rippled out from the floor and crawled upward, setting chandeliers bouncing and knocking pictures off the wall.

"What would you prefer, Skyler?" Jason demanded exasperatedly. "Run for cover down there in the mouth of hell? I don't know about you, but I'm taking my chances out there. Now, go!"

"What about you two?" Scott called as he herded the others out.

"We'll be right behind you."

56

The incessant droning vibrated deep into Shade's bones and the sword in her hand, still so heavy and awkward, resonated with that dreadful vibration as well, as if it were coming alive. Still, she kept slicing away at the near-endless stream of shadows.

"Karen, cover us!" she cried back through the roaring hum. "I'll try to get to Matt!"

The Repha'im darted past with incredible speed. Shade felt sharp claws and beaks stab at her as she fell to her knees by Matt's still form.

The air thickened, merged and then divided, replicating itself in a dizzying display of light and color. Like silver dreams, they glistened and glowed with an unworldly vividness. Finally, one part slowed, then coalesced and began breaking away from the larger mass of air that danced in the darkness.

It reached out to Shade, stretching and struggling to assume form.

Shade, with skills foreign to her, bounced the sword in her hand easily. The entity Anath had now achieved a greater synthesis. There was grace as the body and the spirit moved in fluid partnership. The warrior directed the psychic's muscles in skilled gestures, testing the sword for balance.

Shade noted Karen nearby as she struggled to fight off the wraiths. Matt was an unconscious shape at her feet, crimson blood dripping down his face.

Shade searched around the fallen man but it wasn't there.

Where is it? The thought was anxious as she glanced through the fog, dispersing it with her sword. *There!* Not four feet away from Karen was what she sought.

"Throw me the Talisman!" she ordered. "When it is time, Asherah, I will speak the words."

Karen nodded as she tossed the clay vessel to Shade who caught it expertly. Deep in a corner of her own mind, Shade could observe what was happening, as if watching a play.

She marveled at finding her body moving in ways so totally alien. At the same time, she was aware of the entity's thrill at once more breathing, touching, and feeling.

The warrior in her scanned the surroundings, speared the sword into the ground, and stood poised to renew the battle.

"Host of Seven, now diminish!" Her voice boomed like the eruption of thunder. The words bounced and echoed compellingly into the deepest belly of the cavern.

The swooping blackness grew more agitated. Raucous screams of complaint winged out of the dark. Their resistant cries filled the chamber as harshly as the humming had earlier.

A foul stench of death and corruption spread like a cloud across the chamber. Shade coughed under the onslaught.

She glanced over to Karen, seeing the shadows spiral around her head. However, Karen seemed unaware of their presence. Was she feeling Asherah posses her as completely as Shade had now been given over to Anath?

It is time! We are one!

Voices mingled, echoing strangely in the cavernous space.

"Ashkim, mehr Anath! Ashkim mehr Asherah! Yit besh birkin sahm 'El gezir!"

I summon you, warriors of Anath! Shade thrilled at suddenly understanding the ancient words.

She knelt to the ground, pouring the remaining viscous liquid from the flask.

"Ishk Mot, sunum persh!" She shouted, now knowing the words meant: *The oil of Mot has been poured....*

Shade raised the sword. "Herrub b'besur tisteen."

I set my sword to its task!

"Host of Seven, diminish beneath the Sword of Anath, the Sword of Asherah and the Word of the Priest!" Shade-Anath shouted the command with the ferocity of a warrior.

The swirling shadows gave another pain-filled shriek in response to her harshly uttered commands.

"Tah!"

Go!

For so long they had masqueraded as birds. They struggled to escape the power the words held, but were unable to revert to anything but caricatures of avian horror. The command of the words proved too much of a calling to them; a siren song of destruction. The call snagged them in mid-flight, pulling relentlessly on their ethereal bodies, driving them back, forcing them down, sealing their fate.

57

Jason hurriedly inserted a portable drive and began the download. He had come to terms with losing his equipment, but he'd be damned if he was going to lose all the data. Carrie, meanwhile, moved frantically to salvage what equipment she could.

"Done!" Jason shouted as he tossed the drive to Carrie. She crammed it, along with an assortment of other electronics, into a duffle. Jason slung the bag over his shoulder and grabbed Carrie. With him helping take the weight off her leg, the two dashed into the tempest. Wind slashed and hammered them with debris. A transformer exploded like a super nova, briefly illuminating a wind-savaged main street.

Shocked, Carrie paused for a moment in the eerie glow before Jason lifted her unceremoniously to the shelter.

God help them, she thought.

58

Karen could feel a power surging within the room, as if an electrical charge was about to be released. Whatever was happening seemed to be growing stronger.

She fought back a few straggling Repha'im and then ran over to join Matt and Shade. They clustered protectively around Matt's prone body. She heard again the strangely resonate voice of Shade-Anath.

"Settle, Darkness, into the deepest earthen pit!"

The ground seemed to slither and bulge beneath their feet. Dirt pelted them as the earth shook in protest as if wishing to rid itself of some unwelcome parasite. A hum arose again, not as loud, but more insistent and angry. The sound swirled around the chamber driven by a lashing wind that beat at Karen's body.

Shade raised an arm to her face to deflect the stinging blast of dirty air.

Cradling a still-unconscious Matt, Karen lashed out with the Sword of Asherah.

"Retreat to caves of dust—dwindle down into death," Shade-Anath called out.

The shadows melted and spun giving an angry twist of defiant denial even as it seemed to be forcibly pulled into the crevice of the altar stone.

"Be gone with my final words; be bound by our swords...."

She thrust the amulet high over her head and together they shouted the rest of the incantation.

"Hilka, Hilka!"

One huge column of darkness shot out of the earth in front of the stone altar. It rocketed to the top of the chamber and billowed in a monstrous form before diving with a roar at Shade.

Shade-Anath drew the sword from the ground in one fluid movement. She swung it in a deadly arc that chopped the dark, amorphous form cleanly in half.

As if with one voice, they spoke: "Hilka, hilka, besha, besha! Kakama! Amanu! TAH!"

The ground gave one last climatic shudder as a bellowing channel of hot thick air surged up like a geyser from the crevice. The dry air ripened as it leeched heat and light from the chamber. The air glistened as if growing moist; it twisted, and churned itself into a vile and oily shape.

Shade's mind longed to skitter away from that dark mass but Anath pushed her on.

Part hand, part claw, blistering and thick, the boiling air swept across the chamber lashing out one final time, before it was ripped back into the earth.

The altar tottered and then spider cracks skidded out across its surface like lightning. Another rumble from deep in the earth broke it into a thousand pieces.

The silence that followed seemed as deafening as the din earlier and Shade's ears ached from the total lack of sound. Matt moaned and began to struggle to his knees.

Satisfied that it was over, the Shade-Anath being turned to Karen. The Anath figure and Shade briefly separated and then fused together once more like a double exposure.

Karen's head began to ache at the struggle to keep the figures in focus. She saw the Shade-Anath stoop down to open Matt's hand. The recombinant being gently laid the ancient medallion in his palm and closed his fingers. Then she turned to Karen.

"Make sure the Yellow Wolf keeps this safe. So much has been lost." The Shade-Anath sighed as she glanced at the shattered remains.

"Anath...." Karen began. "She was like a goddess." She could already feel Asherah leaving her.

"No, never that!" the woman gave a throaty laugh. "You must listen carefully to what I say and what I," a hand gently touched Karen's forehead, "show you in here."

"Even as the Wolf's line guarded the knowledge so bravely and so well over eons of time, so much has been lost. So much... Remember this, the ceremony traps the Repha'im, the talisman is needed to bind the creature, and our swords are used to drive it back. The ritual maintains the barrier only for a short time."

"That's why it had to be done over and over."

"Yes. Without all the elements, the force would easily worry the barrier until it broke free once more."

"Ben said they had lost much in the early years. I guess it's a wonder they were able to do anything at all."

"The ritual works best when each element is in balance," Anath agreed. "The most important knowledge they lost was that it couldn't be done alone."

Karen saw the eyes of the woman sadden as she contemplated what had not been in many millennia.

"Wise woman, you must tell the Wolf this: He must embrace not only his past but his future. Without..." the words slurred a little. "Tell him... this...tell him...."

Voice faltering, Shade's body slumped to the ground.

"No! Oh, God!" Karen scrambled up. "Shade, can you hear me? Shade!"

When her head lifted at last, Karen saw once more the Shade she had come to know. My God had it really been only hours since they had met?

"Did it work?" Shade croaked as she struggled to sit up.

A threatening rumble shook the ground and dirt showered down on them.

"It worked." Karen told her helping the other woman to her feet. "Oh, man, did it work!"

59

Like divers bobbing to the surface Shade, Karen, and Matt gasped for breath as they scrambled out of the kitchen.

Running through the lobby they heard hail, hard as pebbles, beating against the windows while a fierce wind rocked cars on the street.

"Hurry!" Karen urged as the building shuddered and something immense collapsed nearby.

Pushing out through the doors, the trio burst into havoc. Icy pellets bombarded them as they glimpsed a wicked rain-wrapped funnel ravenously gunning for the hotel, chewing up Main Street in the process. Debris swirled in cyclonic force like deadly missiles flung in a tantrum of rage.

The fury that had raged within the heart of the great mound had been unnervingly mirrored on the surface. The storm that had first appeared, as if in summons to the waking evil, had finally erupted in monumental fury, striking the old hotel with savage intensity. It was as if Mother Nature herself had come to the fight.

Dodging projectiles hurled at them by the vicious winds, the trio looked frantically for anywhere that might offer them shelter.

Just then, Jason emerged from the side door of the old theater. He motioned frantically for them to hurry.

"There!" Matt yelled above the noise.

As they dashed across the road, Shade glanced up at the swirling wall of destruction. *My God*, she thought. *The hotel will be leveled.*

"There she goes!" yelled Matt over the roar. He shoved them through the door that Jason held open.

Complaining and screeching, the hotel bore the brunt of the massive twister's assault. Like a boxer in the clinch, the old building teetered as blow after blow sent a hail of bricks tumbling to the street.

60

The rain lessened, as the clouds pushed further east and a faint smudge on the horizon heralded the dawn of a new day.

"What a mess," Matt said quietly, almost to himself, as he and the others emerged from the shelter. "I hope no one else in town was hurt."

"Hell of a night, huh?" Shade stared at the tattered remnants of Corvus Mound's historic downtown.

The faces of those still in the rubble rose in her mind.

A cold wind slashed across Shade and she shivered under its sudden assault. She pushed her hair back from her face as she looked to the skies.

Strong winds still flicked the trees like fans but the storm was now miles to the northeast, rushing away in a murky, huddled mass. Ominous rumbles and sparking lights in its core hinted that it had not yet spent itself entirely.

To the east, a faint smudge of daylight was edging up the dark sky. "It all seems so unreal." Shade spoke absently into the silence that grew to fill the spaces between them.

"Poor Peter." Carrie said. Sobbing softly, she buried her tears in Scott's shoulder.

Shade looked around at the scene and took a deep breath of the fresh, if a little damp, night air. The idea of a hot shower, after the last few hours, made her almost giddy. Even better, the headache that had been her constant companion the last few days was gone. Maybe a few days of psychic-free relaxation were in her future.

"This is unbelievable!" Shade groaned as she poured another cup of coffee. She stared at the countertop television in Karen's kitchen. Matt and Jason had stayed downtown to help the local police and rescue teams. Scott had helped Cookie with Carrie and they had just called from the hospital to say the girl's leg would be fine.

As Karen came out of the bathroom Shade called to her. "Karen! You have to see this!"

On the screen, a familiar, if somewhat bedraggled, figure scowled at the camera.

"Come on! Are we live yet? Talk to me!"

Taking a deep breath, Skyler faced the camera, her back to an apocalyptic landscape.

"This is Skyler Dunworth-Michaels, News 6, with an exclusive live report from the devastation left after a massive tornado ripped through this historic community in eastern Oklahoma. All around, an army of heroic volunteers struggles to—"

Karen shut the TV off with a disgusted flourish.

"It's true, after all." Shade said.

"What?"

"Cats—even those with acrylic claws—really do have nine lives." With the sound of Karen's laughter in her ears, Shade headed upstairs toward a hot shower.

As the hot water pelted her battered form, Shade slumped exhaustively down to the tub, resting her head against the wall. It was the longest time before she realized the hot water had run out. Yet, to her it seemed as if she had only just stepped in, as if time had no meaning.

Standing up, she shut off the water, reached for a towel, and picked up the clothes Karen found for her. Slowly, she felt more human again. She finished drying her hair, tossed aside the damp towel, and reached for her dog collar.

Pausing, she glanced at herself in the mirror. Washed away was the heavy mask of Goth makeup. Staring back at her instead was a woman, battle weary but alive, whom she hardly knew.

This one wears protection when she needs none.

The voice echoed in her mind, a wisp of remembered conversations. Comments between two entities that walked between the worlds.

In a cold gray rain twelve years ago Shade had been born and now, in a torrential squall, she had been reborn. *Was that what life was all about? A series of transformations?*

Outside, the sun climbed above the horizon into a clear blue morning, the trees swayed in the cool breeze. Here and there, songbirds could be heard trilling the start to a new day.

Shade took one last look at the leather collar and dropped it into the wastebasket.

EPILOGUE

On the patio outside, Matt watched the traffic pass through the intersection near The Mont. He, Karen, and Shade decided to hold a long-overdue reunion at the bustling bistro, just off the University of Oklahoma campus.

It was a brilliant September afternoon: a cobalt sky contrasted sharply against leaves that had already begun turning warm, golden shades despite the lingering heat of summer.

The architect found it hard to accept the Shade now seated before him, sipping a glass of wine. Hers was nearly the face of a stranger. Gone was her formerly extreme appearance, and in its place, flourished a fascinating blend of strength and beauty.

She wore an expensively tailored, almost anachronistic blouse beneath a vaguely nineteenth century oxblood corset that framed the contrast between her alabaster skin and her now-naturally chestnut hair, which was nearly as dark as the old black dye-job. What he first took to be ornate sunglasses, he now noted oddly were old-fashioned welding goggles.

Gone, too, were the pentagrams, ankhs, skull rings and other trappings of a mall-rat goth. In their place, Shade simply wore an old—almost ancient—bronze ring struck with the image of some warrior goddess. Anath, he guessed.

Karen, too, had changed—in subtler ways. She was still that all-American girl next door, but she'd shed some of the mousy academic. Her bare arms were toned, showing signs of having been digging in the sun all summer. She exuded a new confidence and, he would gladly admit, a sensuality she hadn't before possessed. Previously she had been a cute, if somewhat unsure, girl; now she was a strong, sexy woman.

Have I changed, he wondered. *How must I look to them?*

Matt pushed away the remains of his meal with a sigh. The scorching heat was now fading into a soft, warm evening. The misting devices were just beginning to cool the tables on the outdoor patio.

He had been so busy running Renewal Concepts that his only communication with Karen or Shade had been sporadic posts on Facebook.

"How long are you going to be here, Matt?" Karen asked, as she accepted a drink from the server.

"Not long. The last of the loose ends have been tied off." The amount of red tape and paperwork he had plowed through the last few months had been daunting. "I'm meeting a guy in London next week about restoring several old row houses."

"I love London," Karen effused. "Well, I'm glad our schedules could mesh like this."

"Been a little busy, Karen?" Shade asked with that Mona Lisa grin. "Every time I turn on the TV, I see you on National Geographic, Discovery, the History Channel...."

"Our very own celebrity!" Matt chuckled. "Has that one professor gotten over it yet?"

"As I understand it, he's still whining about fraud. Fortunately, the teams from Chicago and Harvard are helping settle the matter." Karen commented with a gleam of satisfaction. She had really enjoyed those confrontations. It was vindication with a dash of payback. "It seems though that each new find brings up more questions than answers. We're going to be studying and arguing over this stuff for years."

"What about the swords?" Matt asked apprehensively.

Karen and Shade shared conspiratorial glances.

"They're safe." Karen assured him.

"Okay," Matt chuckled. "I trust you guys. The less I know the better!"

"Anyone heard from Jason?" Karen asked.

"I read on their website that he's in Louisiana." Shade offered. "He has been working with the State Bureau of Investigation down there tracking a cult with Satanic ties."

"So he's back to being a cop?" Matt asked.

"I think it's just a consultant job."

"What about his company?"

"He put Carrie in charge of Williams Investigations for now. She, Richard and the new team are analyzing the data compiled at the hotel. Apparently, they're finding some solid scientific evidence in support of supernatural phenomena."

Karen frowned. "I wonder why he decided to step down. It seemed like his passion in life."

"I think," Shade began, pausing for a sip. "Part of him feels like he lost someone else to paranormal beliefs, which makes what he experienced all the more confusing. I think he's still not ready to accept it all—but he's getting there."

Shade had sensed an emotional exhalation in the man when they had last seen one another. But while he may have been on the road to putting his wife's death behind him, he now had the fresh wound of Peter's. In time, Shade knew, he would be all right, but there were still things he needed to work out.

"I hope," Matt spoke, "he finds a way to bridge those two worlds."

"You've made some changes, I see." Karen said, indicating Shade's new look.

"Yeah," she laughed, "I guess after being connected to Anath, I felt different. I don't know, maybe less guarded. I don't feel the need to hide behind a thorny exterior."

"But you've still got a fairly dramatic style," Karen pointed out.

"Yeah," Shade admitted. "Like many of us, I think I built my walls from what was around me. Deep down, I am innately a dark, sardonic soul. I mean, if it weren't for her own demons even Martha Stewart would probably be just a normal fussy housewife."

"I know what you mean," Karen agreed. "Being in touch with those women changed me too. I felt more powerful, confident. For the first time in my life, I didn't feel like I had to run from either my professional critics or my personal foibles. I think it has shown, too. My life has only gotten better since."

Shade nodded, "I feel like there is a light shining on me, in me, through me…. For the first time in a long, long time, I feel good."

"Well," Karen encouraged, "your story isn't over. There is more ahead for you."

Shade looked at her quizzically. "How do you know?"

"I—I don't know. Maybe there is still a part of me in touch with that other reality. Maybe I can still see a bit of what Anath and Asherah saw. I just know with unparalleled certainty that your story isn't over."

Shade stared blankly for a moment, playing with her fork absent-mindedly. Then, with an all too familiar grin, she said, "I think you're right."

"So, Matt." Shade tossed out, eager to shift the conversation away from her. "How is it being the great and powerful Wizard of OZ?"

"I'm coping," he told them. "Getting to know my grandfather in the process. That alone is a good thing."

Matt knew it would be a long time coming before it would be necessary to perform another ritual. *Hopefully*, he thought, *by that time I'll be better prepared.*

"They're tearing the whole thing down, you know," Karen added with a sympathetic glance to

Matt. She suspected he was still sensitive to the pending demise of what he had worked so hard to restore. "Once they've cleared the remaining debris, we can begin our full analysis of the site."

"I expected as much. Donaldson offered me salvage considerations." Matt noted Shade's frown, "but I said no thanks."

"Is that safe?" Karen asked. "I mean, shouldn't it be burned and the earth salted or something?"

Shade seemed about to say something when a series of harmonic chirps interrupted. Excusing herself, she slid from the table, returning a few minutes later.

"Sorry about that," She apologized as she slipped her phone back into her jeans.

"Something wrong?" Karen asked with a look of deep concern.

"No. Just need to track down a serial killer. Nothing big."

NOTES & ACKNOWLEDGEMENTS

Although many aspects of this novel are based on real facets of Oklahoma's past and present, it is entirely a work of fiction and the authors have taken more than a few liberties with history, mythology, and geography.

The Montford Arms hotel, for instance, is a composite of many historic hotels the authors have had the pleasure of visiting, chiefly the Skirvin in Oklahoma City.

No doubt, many readers will be struck by the similarities to that grand hotel. Ironically, the concept of refurbishing the Montford Arms came about long before the actual restoration of the Skirvin.

We have taken ideas of ancient and diverse migrations, the age of ancient human society, and bent them gently to suit our alternate and fictional reality. However, exciting new discoveries in archaeology are constantly challenging older theories and preconceived notions about ancient civilizations.

The Corvus Mounds do not exist; but if you wish to visit their inspiration, we urge you to check out Spiro Mounds State Park near Spiro, Oklahoma. These ancient Mississippian mounds offer a fascinating glimpse into the Pre-Columbian cultures of that state.

Readers may also note familiar motifs running throughout this narrative. This is neither happenstance nor derivative; rather, this is a deliberate attempt to pay homage to the many novels, films, and TV shows that have engendered a love of the supernatural in the authors.

Both authors wish to thank all the paranormal enthusiasts, ghost hunters, psychics, writers, and other walkers in a shadowed world we have had the pleasure meeting over the past few years. Among these, special thanks should go to Tonya Hacker, Keith Pyeatt, Sharon Day, and David Berger for their invaluable insight and input during preparation of this novel.

Cullan Hudson is the author of the popular nonfiction work, *Strange State: Mysteries and Legends of Oklahoma*. His short fiction horror story, "The Iron Door" was featured in the 2005 *Red Dirt Anthology* and includes the Karen Houston character. Hudson has traveled the world in search of unexplained mysteries that inspire works like *The Mound* and his forthcoming short fiction collection, *Dark West*.

www.strangestate.blogspot.com
www.cullanhudson.blogspot.com

Marilyn Hudson holds degrees in History and Library Studies from the University of Oklahoma and has spent decades in the research and reference field. She has a knack for uncovering forgotten stories that has helped her bring history to life in such nonfiction works as *When Death Rode The Rails* and *Hell's Half Acre*. Her chilling collection of short tales, *The Bones of Summer*, has been well received and contains "Runestone," a prequel to *The Mound* that provides greater insight into the novel's back story. Hudson is currently the Director of Libraries at Southwestern Christian University. She lives in Norman, Oklahoma.

www.marilynahudson.blogspot.com
www.hudsonauthor.blogspot.com

Look For These Other Exciting Titles From Worl Books

Strange State: Mysteries and Legends of Oklahoma
By Cullan Hudson

Oklahoma brims with the unexplained. From Ghosts and UFOs to Bigfoot and Buried Treasure, *Strange State* is the most complete work on unexplained tales in the Sooner State. In this volume are rare accounts available nowhere else, each meticulously researched.

The Bones of Summer
By Marilyn A. Hudson

They lay scattered between the vernal flourish and Winter's icy grasp. These are the Bones of Summer, a collection of short tales to chill readers on even the hottest days. Find out what monsters fear in *Erebus*. Take care in what you wish for in *The Purse*. Revenge escapes death's grip in *When I'm Stronger*.